Sue J. Daniels was born in 1964 in North West London, she is from a strong mix of London's east end and Staffordshire heritage.

Since the age of six, Sue has harboured a deep love of reading and creative writing. She attributes this passion to her father, who taught her to read from the racing pages of his evening newspaper, even before she had started school.

The first book in her trilogy of novellas "The Salvaging of Sonny Chapman" won *Finalist* status in The Best Book Awards 2019 and The International Book Awards 2019. Both follow up books "The Restoration of Sonny Chapman" and "The Journals of Sonny Chapman" won *Finalist* status in The Best Book Awards 2020.

Sue writes bravely, and with honesty in her heart.

For Mike, my rock in every storm……

Sue J. Daniels

The Cubby Hole

Stoneface Publishing Ltd

Lincoln, England.

A CIP catalogue record for this title is available from the British Library.

ISBN 978-1-9161039-8-6 (Paperback)
ISBN 978-1-9161039-9-3 (E-Book)

www.stonefacepublishingltd.com
First published (2020)

Stoneface Publishing Ltd.
Writing Rooms, Main Road
Louth
LN11 7TL

Acknowledgements

A huge thanks, as always, to my beautiful, supportive friends and family and to all those involved in helping me get this new series off the ground.

Special thanks to Angela Sutherland from ACG Designs, for yet another truly awesome book cover. To Phillip Ward from yodacoding.co.uk, for his unbelievable knowledge of all things IT. To Sharlene from theredquill.co.uk Editing and Proofreading Service, without whose help, discussion and dedication, I simply could not complete any of my writing projects.

And extra special thanks for this title in particular, to the brave men and women of the Lincolnshire Police and the Metropolitan Police Forces, for their invaluable knowledge and assistance, and for their patience while answering my endless questions.

Prologue

"Come dance." said the raven
with the darkest eyes.
"Follow me." said the magpie.
"Let me tell you my lies."

So they danced as they walked
And they laughed as they talked.
For in the shadows of the night
The truth was out of sight.

Chapter

1

Holly Knowles had always been afraid of the dark. As a baby, she would cry continuously until her mother realised that, by leaving a small night light on in her room, they could get five or six hours of unbroken sleep.

Now, at seven years old, she was just as afraid. Here, in the dark, the musty dampness invaded her senses and compromised her breathing. She could feel the moisture on the wall to which she was attached by a plastic zip tie. Earlier on, she'd heard a scurrying sound, which had multiplied her fear a hundred-fold.

Holly was barely clothed and what she had been wearing when she was taken two weeks previously, had mostly been removed. Now she'd been left on a mattress on the floor with no sheets or covers. She was cold and she was scared.

The man who had brought her here was a vile human being. She thought she recognised him as one of the dads at her school but she couldn't pinpoint which child he belonged to.

Her ears followed the sound of slow, heavy footsteps above. She heard the rattling of two locks before the light, from a bare, hundred-watt lightbulb, pierced her eyes like a hot spike.

The man, and sometimes the woman, made her do unspeakable things. But it was always he who put her through the worst moments, he did things to her that she instinctively knew were wrong on so many levels. When she had cried after first arriving at the house, the tall woman had slapped her hard across the face. She soon learned to stop crying.

Every time the man came to the filthy room, he would get dressed after he had finished with her. It was only then that she knew it was over, for that time at least. It didn't happen every day, but her anticipation of what was coming kept the fear alive. Sometimes, he would be nice, he would make her sit up and take a little food and water.

And then afterwards, he would tie her back up to the metal ring on the wall with a new black plastic tie. As he left he would turn the light off, leaving her terrified and alone in the darkness.

Alone in that darkness, Holly thought about her mother, Heather Knowles. She'd been a young carer for her mum ever since her father had abandoned them and she'd become big enough to fetch and carry. Heather had multiple sclerosis which had forced Holly to have a strength and maturity way beyond her years. She wondered who would be looking after her mother now and how worried she would be. The very thought made her cry deep, mournful tears.

Holly had good support from a local young carers group called 'Pair the Care'. Since being a member, she had learned not to take on such guilt about her mother's illness. She had recently started to enjoy normal childhood activities such as after school clubs and days out with the other children, while the support facilitators took over the lion's share of her mother's care.

Chapter

2

Detective Inspector Rochelle (Rocco) Raven was well-liked within her team in the Galaxy Unit. She'd been blessed with glossy, sleek black hair and the darkest eyes. Now at thirty-six, she was divorced and living alone in her deceased parents' old windmill, which had been bequeathed to her in their will.

Albie, her eight-year-old son, lived with his father most of the time. Michael (Mike) Raven, a medically retired army officer, had all the time and money needed to give Albie everything he needed, while his ex-wife pursued her much-loved career in the police force.

Rochelle's relationship with her ex-husband had tentatively improved over the last couple of years. She had Albie whenever she could. He had a huge bedroom and playroom at the mill and he loved being with either his mum or dad. There was no animosity between them as they always put his needs first.

Rocco had one younger brother called Conrad, who had outed himself as a vibrant gay in his early teens. He was confident and self-assured and, now at the age of thirty-two, he was in a civil partnership with Martin Marshall. They could have formally married but both decided they were happy as they were. Rocco was very close to both Conrad and Martin, as well as her sister Niamh, who was thirty-four. They spent as much time as possible together. The siblings were very close, always trying to replicate their indoctrinated Irish heritage family values. They had keys to each other's houses and happily helped themselves to each other's fridge contents and cupboards.

Rocco was indeed married to her job and although the work in the missing children unit was demanding, both physically and emotionally, she loved it. She enjoyed the way that her team gelled, their confidence, and their ability to detect and trawl through social media with commitment and utter relentlessness. Their enthusiasm and dedication to each and every detail involved in finding the target child, took precedence over everything else in their lives until that case was completely closed.

The Galaxy Unit was relatively new to the Crachenshire Police Force. It had been established two years previously, specifically to work on cases involving child abduction, kidnap and murder. Rocco had been instrumental in setting up the team. She interviewed any potential team applicants, developed the administrative support systems, and project managed case delegation to her specialist team.

Rocco's second-in-command, Sergeant Stacey Lord, had been promoted to her current rank eight months previously. She was a seasoned detective who had been in the force for fourteen years in various roles related to sexual offences. She specialised at working with victims and their families. Having completed a stint in the forces new project, a sex offender management and rehabilitation programme called "Your Turning Point". She had quickly realised that she hated that aspect of sexual crimes work. Her focus and loyalty was, and would always be, to the victims.

At thirty-two years old, she'd been born in Hammersmith, London to hard-working, English shop worker parents. They had invested highly in her education to give her the best possible opportunities in life and she was eternally grateful for that. Her wife Heidi, ten years her junior, was her solace after having lost her parents in a fire at their house, her childhood home. Stacey and Heidi had beautiful twin boys, produced by IUI (intrauterine insemination) on the first attempt.

Stacey had excelled at interview. She was proving to be a hard worker and completely committed to the job and especially her new role within the Galaxy team. Within no time, she had settled in the large open-plan office.

Maggie Seed had also excelled at interview and had successfully bagged the post of administration support lead to the team. She had already been working in the MAPPA (Multi-Agency Public Protection Arrangements) unit of the force for twenty-three years. At fifty-one years old, she was extremely competent and experienced at her job, as well as a welcome supplier of home-baked biscuits, chocolate brownies and monthly cakes. She also provided and stocked the fridge with copious amounts of each member of the team's favourite food. Rocco had munched on celery stalks since giving up cigarettes and was partial to salted popcorn.

Maggie was always first in and last out. She had no one to go home to these days. Her husband had left her for his secretary, where he had worked as the Chief Executive Officer at the Department of Work and Pensions. They had left the area to make a love nest in the south of England.

Nowadays, her beloved cats kept her company in 'Divorcee Land'. She was generally happy, having been awarded the house, the contents and half of her husband's pension in the divorce settlement. Maggie had an excellent memory, hilarious sense of humour and was truly the heart and soul of the team.

Police Constable Mahesh (Hesh) Cole was another member of the team. His mother had originated from India, his father from Norfolk. Extremely vain, he never missed an admiring glance when he passed a reflective window or a mirror. He was particularly good looking, with emerald green eyes and a beautiful olive complexion. He was helpful and respectful to everyone whether they were cleaners in the office or the top brass. His overriding respect included his colleagues and those he worked with on the streets, whether they were criminals or victims. He liked everyone.

He loved his job and was known for his methodical record and timekeeping. He had been in the police force for just under eleven years. He had been determined to get a position in the Galaxy Team and had been successful on his second application. At twenty-eight, he was the same age as his wife Lilian. They had two small children, whom they adored.

Amrita, his mother, was still grieving the loss of her husband five years earlier. She had come to live with them following their invitation. He liked to regale the team with anecdotes about her unbelievably bad habits, especially her table manners. It was not uncommon for her to spit out any food she didn't like, while still seated at the table.

Police Constable Mark Walsh had made it into the team because of his knowledge and vast experience of working in both the Missing Persons unit as well as the CEOP (Child Exploitation and Online Protection) unit.

He was a wizard with social media and had, in his five years of being in the force, systematically trawled through enough child sexual images and sickening images of children in the name of his job, to psychologically destroy any normal human being.

It was Marks commanding officer who had encouraged him to seek a change and find a different role. Mark was from the Caribbean. At thirty years old, he was intelligent, funny and loved by everyone. He had the most beautiful dreadlocks and always smelled gorgeous. Even the male officers would inhale deeply whenever they were around him.

Following his interview, Rocco had insisted that Nate Bridges be employed, purely because of his internet and social media skills. He was not a police officer but ex-army and had joined the force as a civilian eight years earlier.

Twelve years before joining the police, his eleven-year-old sister had been killed by a paedophile, a long time neighbour who'd lived four houses down the street. Nate had been eighteen at the time of the murder, yet the deep feelings of hatred and the need for revenge had never left him. Many times, while in the army, he had gotten himself in difficulty due to his venting his anger in inappropriate ways. A loyal and well-meaning officer had befriended him, teaching him that his vengeful attitude and behaviour was completely pointless in the real world. On one occasion, the officer told him that these all-consuming actions were the same as drinking poison and expecting the perpetrator to die. It had been a lightbulb moment for Nate.

The officer had told him that he would be better served using his knowledge and skills to stop it ever happening again. He encouraged further training and to apply for jobs such as the one he had been successful in getting within the police force.

On leaving the army he had become part of an online vigilante group, hunting down the groomers of young children. Whilst working for one of these groups, which was aptly named 'Paedo Hunters' he learned a particularly valuable skill, which was how to explore the dark side of the internet. He was successful in exposing four different paedophile rings in just eighteen months.

Nate's skill at cracking rainbow tables and working with password hashes was a completely different skill set to the rest of the team, one which the team desperately needed if it had any chance of making a real difference.

Rocco first encountered Nate at the front desk of the police station where she had then worked as a sergeant. It was one gloomy evening when he had brought in evidence that he'd collected. The other desk sergeant booked it in but was oblivious to its true value.

Overhearing what was going on, Rocco, who was just on her way out, asked him to go through to the interview room with what he had. There, he sat with her as she painstakingly read through it all, logging every piece of evidence with the greatest of care. Nate very quickly became a respected source of information for The Galaxy Team. Rocco wanted him on the inside. It didn't take long for him to settle in and become one of the most important and valued members of the team.

The core team worked well together, handling between ten to thirty cases at any one time. Many of the files contained cases of missing teenagers who had run away because of parental neglect, violence, sexual abuse, stepfamily dynamics or a combination of factors.

Sadly, there were many cases involving toddlers and young children who had been taken by warring, divorcing parents, trying to get one over on the other by taking the children abroad and away from the UK legal system without a court application or parental consent.

The hardest to deal with by far, were those children who were taken randomly by strangers for sexual exploitation, trafficking or sometimes to replace a lost child. Fortunately, these cases were rare and, up until now, Rocco could count those cases on one hand. However, all that was about to change for all of them, forever.

Chapter

3

Richard Murphy, thirty-nine years old, had spent a significant amount of time in prison for child sexual assault and molestation. He didn't have a gender preference. His obsession was with children and the absolute power that he commanded over them and how the feelings of power and invincibility surged through him each time he chose to abuse them.

While under arrest, the police had found nine hundred sickening images of children on his phone and even more on his laptop and IPad. While in prison, he had lost an eye when a raging father of six, who happened to be his cellmate at the time, rammed a dessert spoon handle into it.

That same year, he had been successful at his latest parole hearing and had been released On Licence with conditions, including a lifetime listing on the sex offenders register and a commitment to attend three weeks on a sex offender management and rehabilitation programme, designed to ensure that he kept out of trouble and to stop him from re-offending.

He had been closely monitored by the local authorities and the allocated sexual assault and violent offenders' officer. As far as everyone was concerned, he had been doing well, keeping his hands and thoughts to himself. That changed when a particularly smart Sex Offenders Monitoring Officer called Ashley Aldus made an unannounced visit. During the relaxed and quiet visit, Ashley asked Richard if he had offended in any way or if he had been viewing any illegal material.

Richard stated that he hadn't. Just out of the blue, Ashley said he was going to take a look around and randomly discovered a tiny Sim card stashed into the side of a plant pot. With his skilled, expertly trained eye, Ashley had spotted the little gold strip at the top of the card poking out from the soil. On formal investigation, the card was found to contain two thousand indecent images of children.

Richard Murphy was sentenced to a further twenty months in prison. He served nine of those and was given early parole. Once on the outside, he lived in a halfway house for eight weeks until he disappeared from the monitoring radar. He moved to another town, finding a haven in a disused forester's house in a place called Callachen Woods.

Initially squatting in the house, he quietly worked on it to make it a warm and safe home. On discovery, the landowner, pleased with his efforts but unaware of his criminality, offered Richard a legal tenancy. Deep pink hollyhocks, soft blue Canterbury bells, lush golden marigolds, purple foxgloves and several varieties of clematis framed the house and filled the borders with colour and scent, creating an inviting but humble abode.

Richard laboured with his runner bean tripods in thick half barrels. His hanging baskets bore only fruit or small tomatoes. He had made the old house into a chocolate-box scene of joy and rural serenity. A modern-day Hansel and Gretel cottage, indeed.

Growing vegetables and fruit trees and managing a small flock of chickens gave him all he needed to be self-sufficient. Each month he walked to the local shop at the village green, purchasing enough vacuum packed and frozen meat, flour, cheese and supplies to see him through.

Thickset and muscular, Richard filled his five-foot, five-inch body well. Prematurely grey with tortoiseshell spectacles tinted just enough to hide his synthetic eye, he gave the appearance of being just an ordinary guy living a somewhat solitary existence.

Such was his ordinariness, walkers with their dogs and families were always happy to wave and speak to him as they passed through the woods. He was only ever known as Murphy because of his soft Irish accent. While friendly with adults, he always avoided talking to or looking at the children as much as possible.

He'd been through three different sex offender programmes during his time in prison. He ticked the right boxes, played the right games and convinced the facilitators into believing he was a reformed character. When they had let Richard out, he had been prescribed medication to contain his sexual urges. He'd taken some of them when he'd first been released, but over time had convinced himself that his urges would diminish naturally and that just the thought of ever going back inside would keep him regulated enough. Nevertheless, he kept a small stash hidden at the back of his medicine cabinet.

On the 6th April at 10:15hrs, all of that changed when he heard little Leon Dalton, an eight-year-old boy, crying in distress, just outside his house in the wood. Heart racing, blood pumping, his brutal, depraved sexual urges returned to him like a speeding train. Gone were any inhibitors of his deviant behaviour.

With controlled breathing and articulate precision, his head and neck standing tall, pushing out his chest of his five foot, five inch body. He calmly went outside to comfort the small boy.

Chapter

4

Harris Evans woke up and found that his blue rimmed glasses were broken. He wanted his mum and dad and his toy dog called George. He was laying on a hard floor and he didn't feel very well. The floor beneath him was cold and wet and he was dizzy. He tried to stand but his legs buckled. It felt like the time he and his friends had tried some of his dad's whiskey. Managing to sit up, he took his coat and jumper off. He put his coat back on and made a pillow out of his jumper. His head was hurting even more as he huddled alone in the darkness.

Harris dreamt of a man and a woman asking him to get into their car. He could see that they had two black puppies on a white blanket in the back of their green Ford. While most other boys loved cars or football or trains, Harris Evans loved dogs. His whole world revolved around them and he spent hours and hours just drawing all types of dog. He told anyone who would listen that one day when he was grown up, he would have a job working with dogs.

When they had asked him to get into their car because they needed someone to look after their puppies for just a little while he didn't think for a second about the hundreds of '*stranger danger*' warnings that his parents and the school teachers had drummed into him, time and time again. But these two were elderly, like his grandparents. They were smiling and warm and safe and friendly, not monsters, like the ones he had been warned about. It was as if they knew about his love for dogs.

Harris woke with a start. He realised that it hadn't been a dream after all. It was real, very real and it had happened to him just six hours ago. He cried until, exhausted, he fell back to sleep.

He was startled awake when the big door opened. He was grabbed by a man who stank of sweat, beer and cigarettes. He recognised the smell because his dad sometimes took him to the local pub on a Sunday and some of the old men in the toilets had the same smell.

Harris couldn't see properly. He felt disorientated without his glasses. He felt himself being carried by the huge putrid man into a larger, brightly lit room. He could just make out that there were more men sat in a circle of chairs. The elderly woman who had taken him was there too. They stared at him as the woman undressed him down to his trousers.

'Get him bathed, Gloria. He stinks. We want him smelling nice to meet the buyers when they come to window shop before the auction. Feed him and sort out his eyes. What's wrong with them?' asked the huge man.

Harris took his broken glasses from his pocket and showed them to the man they called Lance. His little hand was shaking, which brought a sinister smile to the man's face.

'Well, we don't want to worry about that, young man. We have lots of children's glasses here. Look in here." grinned Lance.

Lance took Harris's hand as he led him to a drawer which was full of glasses of all colours.

'Take your pick, young man.' laughed Lance.

Desperate to see clearly, Harris quickly chose a green pair and tried them on. As he turned around, he could feel hot urine running down his leg. There were children, many children, in chairs, each bound with a rope. Two little girls were looking straight through him. Their vacant expressions made them appear lifeless as if their souls had already left their bodies.

'Annie, get here now!' shouted Gloria, Harris quickly recognised her as the bossy woman who had taken him and brought him to this place.

A gangly teenager came running obediently into the room, nodding furiously as her downcast eyes pleaded for forgiveness in case she had taken longer than she was allowed. Harris noticed that she had something wrong with her mouth.

'Get this child washed and find him some decent clothes. He needs feeding, plumping up a bit. We want him looking a bit healthier and fresher for our guests. Now go but hurry up. And remember the rules, girl. Do *not* talk to him, you little bitch.' hissed Gloria, through gritted teeth.

'Yes, Miss!' replied Annie as she led Harris to the kitchen. Annie sat him on a chair at the big wooden table. Busying herself while she boiled eggs, she buttered bread and poured boiling water over the powdery contents of a tub of chicken Pot Noodles. He noticed that the food cupboard was full of Pot Noodles in every flavour.

'What is this place?' whispered Harris to the strange girl, as he looked around in absolute horror.

'You know I'm not allowed to talk to you. Didn't you hear her? Didn't you listen?' she growled a whisper at him.

'I'm sorry. I just don't know how I got here or why I can't go home. I will get into so much trouble for being late home from school.' sobbed the boy as he looked down to the floor.

He ate greedily as they sat in silence. After a while, Annie got up and found him some suitable clothes from a big pantry in the kitchen.

Harris noticed that the house was filthy and there was a distinct odour of something familiar to him. It was like the smell at the bottom of his rabbit cage. It made him feel sick, just like it did when he cleaned out his rabbits.

'Now you've finished eating, let's go and get you cleaned up and dressed in some decent clothes.' said Annie.

'Then will I be able to go home?' pleaded Harris.

Annie looked at the boy with desperate sadness in her eyes. "I don't think you'll be going home, ever again."

Harris was shocked at her words. He silently scanned her face for something, anything that might give away the joke or the lie, maybe some tiny thing. A tell in her eyes, maybe. He couldn't see anything and in that very moment, he knew she was telling the truth. He started to howl like a wounded animal.

The sound of footsteps echoed like thunder along the passage to the door of the filthy kitchen. The woman he now knew as Gloria, grabbed Annie's arm and slapped her hard across the face again and again.

'What did I tell you, you useless little bitch? No talking to them or you'll be back in that room with the men as you were before, ugly or not. Do you hear me?'

'Yes, Mrs Mountford, I hear you.' whispered Annie, handprints glowing on her face.

'Now, get him ready and make sure that you bring him back to the drawing-room at eight o'clock sharp. We have a couple coming to preview.' shouted the woman as she glared from Annie back to Harris.

'Now, do you see what I mean? They are cruel like this all the time. It's best to just do as they say and you might get to live.' she whispered to Harris.

'But who wants to live like this. I just want to go home.' the boy cried.

Chapter

5

Richard had found a small brown terrier dog called Sukie. She was an old dog and he thought she must have just been brought to the wood and abandoned. He had also discovered a small room at the back of the old forester's cottage, which appeared to have been used for storing old tools. He had kitted it out with a single iron bed and a variety of toys. There was a full train track set on the concrete floor. He'd even tacked colourful posters on the crumbling wall. Well, just in case.

The spare room wasn't visible from inside the rest of the house as the door was covered up by a huge oak dresser that Richard had painstakingly upcycled when he had first squatted there. He had since bricked up the back entrance which was now concealed by the beautiful glistening green leaves of his Boston Ivy creeper. He smiled to himself as he thought about the saying 'Finder's Keeper's'. He had every intention of keeping this little find for himself.

Sitting him down at the kitchen table, Richard asked the boy if he was hungry. Between his sobs, the little boy nodded that he was. He greedily ate the bread and butter placed before him and drank a small glass of milk which Richard had laced with enough ketamine to keep him quiet. As the drug took effect, Richard asked if he wanted to play a game. Leon nodded groggily and so Richard started to sing the old nursery rhyme about the body's skeleton.

'Your ankle bone is connected to your leg bone; your leg bone is connected to your knee bone.' touching Leon in the corresponding places on his little body. Leon couldn't help giggling silently, yet couldn't quite grasp what was happening. Richard suggested that it would be better if they moved to a more comfortable room. By now Leon was fading fast. Richard panicked as he thought that he may have given the child a bit too much of the drug.

He'd already moved the dresser in anticipation. As he carried Leon into the room he moved swiftly like some kind of reptile, his tongue flashing in and out of his mouth with excitement. As he quickly laid the now sedated boy on the bed he heard voices outside. Pushing the heavy dresser back in place, he hurried out into the garden, annoyed that he had been disturbed.

'Leon! Leon! Leon, where are you my darling? Mummy is here!' cried a very distressed woman, who appeared to be in her early thirties.

Sophie Dalton kept wailing for her son, as Richard came out of the forester's cottage.

'What on earth is the matter? Are you okay?' enquired Richard, trying to sound comforting and convincingly concerned.

'It's my son Leon. He's gone! I let him out of my sight for a second while I ran to find my dog, and now I can't find him anywhere.' the woman answered in between her sobs.

'Would you like me to help look for him?' offered Richard.

'Oh yes. Yes, please! If you have time that would be a great help.' she pleaded.

'Look, children often go missing around here but they always get found. You know what boys are like. Their imaginations get the better of them playing soldiers. Most often, they just find their way home on their own." said Richard trying to placate her and divert her from his crime. After they had been searching for some time Mrs Dalton spoke again. "Do you think he might already be at home, then? I need to call my husband and then the police." the woman continued in panic.

'Well look. Why don't you just see if he is at home first? I'll keep looking here and if he's not there when you get home then you can call the police and they'll carry out a search for him straight away.'

'Yes, okay. If you don't mind keeping an eye out for him then that's what I'll do.'

Immediately, they began to walk back to the cottage. As the woman sped away, Richard knew that, once the police came with dogs, they'd more than likely find the boy. His boy. He knew what he had to do. His urges would have to wait. If only he could just hide his prize for a little while longer.

He went to the kitchen and, moving the brown and orange striped rug from the middle of the room, he reached down into a hole in the floorboards. He retrieved the secret mobile phone that he'd hidden for emergency use only. He rang his old cellmate, one of the good ones, one like him, one like Lance.

'Hey, ole boy. Is that my old mate Dick Murphy?'

'To what do I owe the pleasure?' asked the gruff voice on the other end of the phone.

'Hi, Lance. Look, I haven't got much time, mate. I've got a nice piece of play here, about eight years old he is. But I need to hide him for a while. Anything you can do for me?' asked Richard Murphy, in desperation.

'You still at that wood?' asked Lance.

'Yeah, sure, still here.' replied Richard.

'Okay, I'll send a delivery truck now with some large garden pots. You know, like the big garden centre ones. Put him in one of those with a lid on and make sure he's drugged properly, right.'

'I'll get him ready now. And Lance, keep him sweet for me!' said Richard.

They both sniggered, each with a pig-like grunt, a revolting sound that would send a shiver through the hearts of most normal human beings.

Chapter

6

It was at 17:15hrs on Thursday, 6th April that the first notification came in from the Operations department. DCI Rochelle Raven took a deep breath as she listened to her colleague Hesh, as he read out the details:

Child Rescue Alert

*Leon Dalton
*Dark Blonde Hair
*Dark brown eyes
*Male – small build
*Eight years old
*Last seen today at Callachen Woods with his mother who had made him wait while she ran off to find their dog who had taken chase of a rabbit.

Realising that time was of the essence, Rocco delegated tasks to each member of the team.

'Right. Hesh, get two officers from the SATS Unit and go to the mother's house. Knock on all the neighbouring houses and start asking questions. I want a statement and I need every detail about this boy. His friends, his school, outside activities, and well, you know the rest.' ordered Rocco.

'Yes Ma'am. We're on it.' replied Hesh.

As he got his gear together, ready to leave the unit, Rocco continued delegating to her team.

'Mark. Nate. I want any social media profiles checked again and again and I want to know everyone he has spoken to in the last twelve weeks.

'Of course Ma'am. We'll get on to it right away.' answered Nate and Mark in unison.

Maggie knocked and opened the door into Rocco's office and said 'Ma'am, I'm sorry to butt in, but there's been another missing child reported.'

Rocco stared in disbelief at her Team Administrator. 'What the fuck is happening here! Mags, let me see that printout.' ordered Rocco, reaching out for the document.

Maggie handed her the sheet of paper.

Child Rescue Alert

*Holly Knowles
*White Blonde Hair
*Blue eyes
*Freckles
*Female – small build
*Seven years old
*Last seen going to the chemist in Chorley Road to collect her mother's prescription.

Falling back into her chair and running her hand through her hair, Rocco read the information and knew immediately that this was going to be a very long day.

'I hope this isn't going to be a serial child abductor. Please God, no.' Rocco prayed to herself, but within earshot of Maggie.

Chapter

7

Rocco answered only to Chief Superintendent Edward Trenchard, who was affectionately known to his family and friends as Trenchie. He was easy-going most of the time. But he had his moments, especially when crimes weren't being solved, meaning that he would be under intense pressure from those above his rank. He managed Rocco and the Galaxy team but kept very much in the background. The Galaxy Unit was only one of the many plates he kept spinning.

Trenchie was a lovable rogue. Tall and muscular, with deep auburn hair and lots of freckles. He and Rocco had a somewhat private romantic history. Clearly, he still held a torch for her as he was never able to get his words out when he was around her. Rocco was well aware of his continued love for her and, without malice, used it to every possible advantage when she needed to get extra resources for her team.

He had, to some extent, been the cause of her relationship breakdown with Mike, not that she had been physical with Trenchie. An intense psychological connection had developed way before they got it together sexually.

Trenchie had been married to Lydia. She had become like a trusty old friend to him. There had been no love or intimacy between them for a very long time. He had decided that this was not the way he wanted to live and just up and left one Sunday afternoon. Their love had diminished long before he had set any sights on Rocco.

When his eyes met Rocco's, whether alone, in the office, or in a room full of people. He still wanted her and he still reminded her of that fact from time to time. Trenchie had never experienced any woman who was so beautiful in every way. He admired models and famous film stars such as Audrey Hepburn, Marilyn Munroe and many more. But Rocco had a natural beauty and softness about her. Even when she wore just running gear, she looked just as gorgeous to him, as when she dressed for work in smart clothes. He thought that one day, he would win back her affections and take her away from the stresses of this job. He would marry her if she would have him. He was prepared to play the long game.

Rocco had finished the relationship with Trenchie after Mike had found out. Even though they had recently separated, it didn't sit well with Rocco.

Mike had taken Albie to the Mill early one Sunday afternoon, as he had a football tournament the next day and needed to be at his Mum's to prepare for it. Trenchie, who was just leaving, met Mike and Albie at the door.

It had been an awkward moment, to say the least. Rocco could see from Mike's expression that he wasn't sure if this had been a visit for business or pleasure. A subtle glance in Rocco's eyes told Mike that it was the latter.

The whole incident had left Rocco in a state of unrest for some weeks. Everyone, both at the Galaxy Unit and Police Headquarters, knew about their affair. No one, not anyone, ever spoke about it.

Entering his office now, Rocco knew she needed back up and extra police officers on the ground.

'Hello Roc, how are you?' greeted Trenchie.

Rocco stood leaning against a filing cabinet with one hand across her body and the other twirling her hair.

'I'm tired Trench. These children going missing is taking its toll on all of us. I hate to ask, but we need more resources. We'll never do it with just the officers we currently have. They are exhausted already.'

'Come and sit down. Let's see what we can work out. Can I get you a coffee?' he offered.

'Yes, please. I'd love one, thank you.' replied Rocco as she sat down at his desk.

Pouring the coffee from the regularly topped-up filter machine, he enquired about her life and whether or not she was happy. It was something he asked her at every opportunity.

'I've not had much time to think about anything else, to be honest. This case has consumed me in every way. You know, just work, sleep, eat and repeat at the moment.'

They sat and chatted for over an hour. He was his usual charming and attentive self. Making her laugh and feel adored. She left his office getting a promise for additional resources whenever she might need them, which gave her a sense of relief, if only for a moment.

Chapter

8

The usual protocol kicked in and the team set about obtaining full details of each of the reported missing children, their friends, movements and establishing the circumstances of how and when they were last seen. Procedure dictated that checks were needed to be made for any risks involved or if the children were being exploited by another party in addition to health, educational and social care histories.

Both of the children's homes were searched as well as any outbuildings. Family members were interviewed. With the search notes and Police National Computer submissions completed, the reports came back to the Galaxy Unit.

There were issues around the missing child Holly Knowles as she was the main carer for her mother. She was bound to have a rebellious streak or, at least, needed a break. Someone suggested that she may not be missing but just taking some time to herself.

Whatever the judgements or assumptions in the briefing room, these children urgently needed to be found. A plan of action for each child was created and distributed.

The Action Plans were recorded on the Force's Command and Control system and subsequent MIsPer information was circulated on the Police National Computer (PNC). Maggie made the notifications to Children's Social Care and a meeting was set up for them to attend the next day.

At the morning briefing, the team gathered around ready to hear the latest on the two MisPers.

'This little Holly Knowles. I wonder if she has just absconded, you know. Kids looking after their sick parents. It must be awful for them. What an absolute burden that must be for one so young?' said Stacey.

'It doesn't matter why she's missing Stacey. She is seven years old and I think it's just a bit coincidental that we've got two missing children within days of each other.' replied Rocco.

Rocco cast her eyes around the room 'Anyone else got any ideas? Any results in yet?' Rocco could see the anxiety and concern on each person's face.

The team was silent. Each of them had their caseloads as well as these two new missing children. There had been no CCTV as yet, nor any reports of suspicious activity. This wasn't a good start.

Rocco always followed the Police Decision-making framework, even though it was known for being complex. The structure had always helped her and she insisted that her team follow the process to the letter. She was well aware that difficult decisions were often required in difficult circumstances. They were often made based on incomplete or generalised, totally contradictory information with little or no evidence.

Nevertheless, she drew on them whenever she needed to. She finished the briefing and sent the team out with more tasks and instructions. She then decided to organise a television news bulletin to help find the two children.

Chapter

9

Police Interview

Sophie Dalton – Personal Account
Present: DCI Rochelle Raven, Sergeant Stacey Lord, Mrs Sophie Dalton.

'Mrs Dalton, thanks for agreeing to talk with us. Can we start by taking you back to last Tuesday afternoon?' asked Rocco.

'I literally left him for seconds while I went to find the dog. It was when I came back to the car that I discovered he'd gone. I honestly thought he was hiding from me.' replied Sophie Dalton.

'At what point did you start to panic, Mrs Dalton?' enquired Rocco.

'I was shouting Leon's name. Screaming, crying like an idiot. To be honest, I was getting annoyed with him because he's always playing games with me.'

'Can you tell us what happened next, Mrs Dalton?' asked Stacey.

'Well, I was losing it big time, I can tell you. I was on my knees, like a child myself. Then out of nowhere, this man appears. He asked me what on earth the matter was, and if I was okay. I explained that my son Leon had just disappeared. I told him again and again that I'd let him out of my sight for just a second while I ran to find my dog and that I couldn't find him anywhere.' replied the shaken and distressed woman.

'Okay, it's perfectly okay to be upset, Mrs Dalton. Take your time. When you're ready, can you tell us what happened next?' asked Stacey, gently.

'So the man, you know, the man from the house in the wood place. He asked if he could help. I think he said something like "Would you like me to help you look for him?" I begged him to help. "Oh yes! Oh yes, yes, please!" I said to him "If you have time that would be a great help!" And he did. He helped me look, for ages. We even looked in his cottage but there was no sign at all.'

'And what did he have to say, Mrs Dalton?' continued Stacey.

'He said something like "Children often go missing but they always get found. You know what boys are like." He said that their imaginations get the better of them and that they sometimes just find their own way home. After we searched for a while, we decided that he might already be at home and so I agreed to go home and call my husband and you lot. The man, I think he's called Murphy, said he would keep looking in the woods with his dog and meet the police when they arrived.'

'Okay. Mrs Dalton, this next bit is very important. The man, the one you called Murphy, can you tell me a bit more about him, please?' asked Rocco.

'Yes, he seemed very nice. He was very helpful. He did his best to reassure me. He helped me when I needed him. We searched for ages before I went home.'

'When you look back to that day, Mrs Dalton, did you see anything or anyone suspicious in the car park? What about during your walk around the woods itself?' continued Rocco.

'No there were a few bird watchers about. But none of the cars were occupied when I got back to the car park.'

'Okay, Mrs Dalton. I can see that you're upset and I can assure you that we're doing everything we can to find your son. Thank you for coming in today. Please call me or my colleague if you think of anything at all that might be relevant. We can conclude this interview for today. Sergeant Lord, can you escort Mrs Dalton to her car, please.'

Sergeant Stacey Lord carried out her chief's instructions. When they got to the car she gestured to Sophie Dalton to wait for a second, before telling her gently 'Just before you go, Mrs Dalton. As you know, the television briefing is set for the day after tomorrow. The media team will be in touch tomorrow and you will, of course, be supported in every way possible.'

Sophie Dalton was beyond exhaustion, bone tired, she hadn't slept much and eating hadn't even occurred to her. She left the police station completely disorientated.

Maggie had arranged for a police car to take her home and to make sure that there was someone with her for a while. She'd also ensured that Mrs Dalton had been given a direct number for the Family Liaison Officer connected to the case.

Laying down on Leon's bed, his favourite stuffed bunny, *Floppo,* writhing in her hands, Sophie sobbed quietly into his pillow. Drifting off, she was soon deep into a dream where she could hear her tiny son calling out to her.

Back at the station, Rocco spoke with Stacey.

'Who conducted the search of that woodman's house and where is he now? I want him in here today. Get Mark and Hesh out there with a search team and lift everything in that house again, and again. We'll do it while he is being interviewed.'

'Yes ma'am, I'll get on to it right now.' replied Stacey, as she quickly made her way out to the main office to task Hesh.

Chapter

10

Stacey Lord knocked on the thick glass window of Rocco's office.

'Ma'am, we've had another report. A third child, the same age range as the other two. I've got a really bad feeling about this.' said Stacey Lord, with a serious look on her face.

'Come on in, Stacey. What have we got?' asked Rocco, holding out her hand, as her second-in- command handed her the latest report.

Child Rescue Alert

*Missing child
*Harris Evans
*Strawberry Blonde Hair
*Blue eyes
*Freckles

*Blue Rimmed Glasses
*Male – small build
*Seven years old
*Last seen on his way home from school.

'What's going on here? They're disappearing fast! So far, all three are a similar age. This is unbelievable!' cried Rocco, in exasperation and fear. A huge knot was beginning to form in her stomach.

'Okay, give me half an hour. We need to set up another briefing in the meeting room. Can you round up the team, please, Stacey.'

By now, Hesh had also appeared at her door, and she immediately tasked him with additional instructions.

The team had gathered and was waiting for Rocco's arrival. She nodded to them in greeting, as she made her way to the front of the briefing room.

The current information was on the investigation board, with links and possible sightings to photographs of each child. Rocco proceeded to address the team.

'Okay. So far, we've got three kids who have gone missing in the space of four days. It's looking more and more like a serial child abduction. We don't know that yet so keep an open mind.

It could just be a coincidence, although that is doubtful. Any information on your follow-ups so far Hesh, Mark, Nate?' enquired Rocco.

Nate stood up and presented everything he had managed to find on the missing girl, Holly Knowles. He noted her excellent school reports and that she was a carer for her mother who had multiple sclerosis. She was very popular at school and loved sports, especially athletics. He stated that she had Facebook and Snapchat accounts, their existence unknown to her mother.

'What's the story with her mother, currently? I mean, does she have someone to care for her?' Rocco asked.

'She has the police liaison officer with her while the search is being carried out and social services have taken up the personal care side of things and she has the full support of "Pair the Care" services.' replied Nate.

'We've already conducted a house to house Ma'am, and both the route from the chemist where she was going to collect her mother's prescription, her school and the grounds are being searched as we speak.' continued Nate.

'Thanks, Nate. Anyone else have anything for us?' asked Rocco.

'Ma'am, the young boy, Leon Dalton, was last seen at Callachen Woods.

He literally just vanished. So far, I've found no witnesses, not even a trace. He was alone with his mother and their dog in the woods. There weren't any other cars parked or dog walkers that the mother can remember, just some old bloke who lives in the forester's cottage.' reported Hesh.

'Has a full search been carried out? Has the old man in the wood been questioned? In fact, is it the same guy I've already asked to be brought in?'

'They had limited resources Ma'am. Twelve search officers and several police volunteers have been assigned to search the area but those woods go on for miles. There must be a thousand acres or more and a lot of it is thick hawthorn bush.' replied Hesh.

'What about the search dogs?' exclaimed Rocco.

'I'll get on to it now, and chase that up Ma'am.' replied Hesh.

Rocco rolled her eyes and shook her head. 'A child is missing in the woods! And we've not sent the dogs in yet! Seriously!' After an exasperated pause, Rocco continued. 'Right. Anyone else with anything to share?'

'I'm sorry I'm late, Ma'am. I've just been talking with a man called Anthony Jerome. He may be a possible witness in the vicinity where Harris Evans went missing. He states that he saw a young boy with an elderly couple and that something didn't quite add up. The witness states that he initially thought it was grandparents with their grandson, but the way the boy was suddenly pushed into the back of the car made him feel uncomfortable.' said Stacey Lord as she took a seat in the meeting room.

Rocco's head went back and her eyes widened. She was impressed with this sudden news. It could be the early breakthrough they needed.

'Right, Stacey. Find your witness and get him back in here today. I want to speak to him myself.'

Chapter

11

Once more, Holly was shaking with fear as she heard the heavy footsteps coming. It was so dark in this place. He was there at the door. She knew it was him, and soon he would be inside the room, hurting her again.

The last few times she found that she was quicker at detaching and watching from above as he did those awful things to her tiny seven-year-old body. Somehow, this seemed to numb her from what he was doing. She didn't know how she did it. It seemed to just happen.

In the beginning, she would count all her cartoon character stickers, over and over again in her mind, or she would think about being with her friends at school.

But since she had started being able to detach herself, the physical pain and the fear seemed less. She didn't seem to have any emotion. It was as if she was looking down on both of them from above, trying to make sense of what was going on as she watched. A strange curiosity. There was this incredible sense of numbness, of nothingness, of floating on the ceiling, as if she was watching a movie of herself.

Suddenly, she heard the unmistakeable ringtone of a mobile phone. It had the same tone as her mother's. The rattling of the door handle stopped and she heard him walking away as he answered the call. 'Hey, ole boy! Murphy, my man!'

At least, that's what it sounded like, but she could be wrong. She was thirsty and disorientated and so very tired. Holly waited, expecting the door to open again and it did, but this time it wasn't the vile man or the old angry woman. It was an older child, a girl about fourteen years old.

'What's your name?' asked Holly.

'I'm not allowed to talk to you.' whispered the girl. She had been told to take food and water to Holly but she had been forbidden to speak to her.

Holly started to cry, a rivulet of tears began running through the dirt that was caked on her face.

'Pleeeaaase talk to me. I'm so scared.'

The girl finished stirring the stinking Pot Noodle. She tore two pieces of bread and placed it and the plastic cup of noodles on the makeshift side table. She sat down beside Holly and, taking her free, hand she held it in her own.

Annie liked this one. She reminded her of herself, and she could sense that she was stronger than the others. She decided that she would take a chance and speak to her. But very quietly.

'Look, you need to eat and you need to keep strong. Stretch your legs every day. Try and move or you'll be too weak because if there's ever a time you can break free, you will need all of your strength. Do you understand me?' whispered Annie.

Holly stared at her. Not a sound came out of her mouth as she watched the girl climb back up the steps. She heard the door lock, leaving her behind in the total darkness.

Just as she was about to nod off, she heard screaming outside the door.

'Annie, get here now, you little bitch. You better not have spoken to that child! Do you hear me?'

Holly recognised the voice as that of the woman who had made her dance like a fairy in the big room when she first arrived. In front of all those people.

Holly ate the Pot Noodle as best she could with one hand by balancing it between her thighs and dipping the bread in. The hot plastic burned her bare skin, but at least that meant that she could still feel.

A new energy began to well up within her. For the first time, she started to think about escaping this horrible dump. Since the older girl had mentioned the possibility, she felt a glimmer of hope that she might be able to get away, to get back to her mother.

Holly was startled from her daydream by the sounds of the girl being viciously slapped. She could hear her pleading with the woman.

'I'm sorry! I'm sorry! I don't talk to them, I swear! Please, please stop.'

Chapter

12

In less than three hours after Rocco had tasked a search, Hesh and Mark had located and brought Richard Murphy into the station for questioning, just as he was about to board a bus at the Callachen Bus Depot. As soon as a Legal Aid solicitor arrived, he was taken into the interview room where Rocco and Stacey were waiting.

DCSI Eddie Trenchard had positioned himself behind the one-way glass. He, too, had a special interest in this suspect.

He had been reading Richard Murphy's arrest record and previous criminal activity. He noted the vast amount of child images, including photos and videos that had been found on his arrest. It was these that were the most revolting and extremely concerning.

Police Interview

Richard Murphy – Potential Suspect

Present: DCI Rochelle Raven, Sergeant Stacey Lord, Mr Richard Murphy, Mr David Marchant (Solicitor)

'Mr Murphy, thank you for coming in. We have some questions that we would like to ask about the disappearance of a young boy around the place of your residence at Callachen Woods. What can you tell us?' asked Rocco.

'Well firstly, I hardly had any choice, did I? It's simple, really. A child went missing and I ventured outside to help look for him. We couldn't find him, so the mother went home in case he turned up there.'

'I've been reading your previous history, Mr Murphy. It's a long and interesting life of criminal activity, isn't it?' offered Stacey.

Dressed in his gardening clothes of light blue shirt, faded corduroy trousers and worn out wellington boots, Richard Murphy appeared dishevelled as he sat with his chin on one hand. Following a nod from his solicitor, the woodsman became frustratingly consistent in his two-word reply. And it was impossible to miss his condescending tone.

'No comment.'

'I put it to you, Mr Murphy, that you do have something to do with the disappearance of this boy and we will find out what that is. It's only a matter of time.' stated Rocco.

'Are you prepared to help us with this serious investigation at all, Mr Murphy? I mean, once we have spoken with the sex offender monitoring team to let them know where you are, maybe you might be a bit more helpful.' suggested Rocco, looking straight into his eyes.

'No comment.'

Richard displayed both annoyance and boredom at the questioning and refused to disclose anything. It was Richard's legal right not to reply. But both Rocco and Stacey knew from the start that this was not the behaviour of an innocent man. Rocco was convinced in the depth of her gut that it was he who had taken the little boy. But Rocco was not ready to give up so easily.

'You don't appear to be very interested in what's happening here, Mr Murphy. But *we are very interested.* The reason we are asking you these questions is that we want to find little Leon Dalton. Every second counts. The longer he is missing, the more chance he is dead. If you are saying this wasn't you, that you've had nothing to do with his disappearance, if it wasn't you who took him, if you really weren't involved and we are speaking to the wrong person, just tell us now. We want to find Leon and not waste time interviewing the wrong people. Do you get that, Mr Murphy?' challenged Rocco.

'No comment.'

'What was it, Mr Richard Murphy? What was it that made you decide to take this boy?'

'No comment.'

'I mean, given your form. You must have been just waiting for the day. The day that would bring you a small boy, like the ones you have taken in the past. The crimes, Mr Murphy, which have already put you in prison for a considerable length of time.'

Rocco was getting more and more annoyed at his 'No comment.' routine. It was time to try a different approach. Trenchie smiled to himself as he watched from behind the observation glass. She was good at this, and he was waiting for the man to break.

'No comment.'

'So come on, was it a planned grab or just an opportunity that you couldn't resist, Mr Richard Murphy? It must have been like Christmas for you- a young boy alone. What an opportunity for someone like you!' goaded Rocco.

'No comment.'

It was clear that this wasn't the first time this man had been under intense questioning. But his demeanour had begun to change. He covered his face in his hands, while intermittently wiping his eyes. He was now constantly fidgeting and was sweating profusely, evident from the stains that saturated his shirt. But he still didn't give anything up. They didn't know if it was fatigue or guilt that had caused the changes? It was time to stop.

After the interview, Richard was released without charge, due to the lack of anything but circumstantial evidence and he smirked at the officers as he left the police station. They had tried to obtain an arrest at the same time, as he was in breach of his parole conditions such as changing his address without notification, but they couldn't make it stick.

He knew that they wouldn't leave him alone now. He also knew that he had no choice but to go to ground as soon as he could, because they could arrest him again for dropping off the Sex Offenders Register radar, as well as being a suspect in one of the most recent child abduction cases. Thank goodness he had managed to get the boy moved so quickly. His old mate, Lance, had come up trumps. He smiled to himself as his tongue flickered over his lips.

Arriving back at his cottage in the wood, he wasn't shocked to find that while he had been at the station being interviewed, the cottage had been taken apart. He was mad about it but he knew he didn't stand a chance of complaining.

They hadn't discovered the room behind the big cupboard. Idiots! Right now, his focus was to get moving as quickly as possible. He was heading to pick up his new boy. He had to get to the auction before the police got to him again for another round of interrogation. Grabbing his backpack, he filled it with what he would need and left the cottage to hitchhike his way out of there.

It wasn't long before a lorry stopped. Running alongside to keep up with its braking distance, he quickly climbed onto the shiny running board and into the cab. Stating his destination, the driver nodded to him. They were silent from then on.

Chapter

13

Clara Thompson loved to ice skate. At such a young age, she was already a junior champion who had won numerous awards.

When she was four and a half, her grandfather, Duke Thompson, took her to the ice rink in the swanky new leisure centre which had been built on the outskirts of Callachen. She had immediately fallen in love and had joined a beginners' skating class on the same day.

As Clara flourished in her newfound passion, her grandfather jokingly remarked that he had struck it lucky to have discovered his granddaughter's love of ice skating.

For Clara, skating was her life. While on the ice, she believed she could do anything. She felt free and happy. Clara was well-liked by her many friends and popular among the boys. She bore a striking resemblance to a very young Naomi Campbell. She was a beautiful child, inside and out.

She practised skating every day after school and even longer on Saturdays. In addition to her rigorous training schedule, she spent most of her free time on the ice, sometimes helping younger children to learn the basics. However, her mother insisted that she rest on Sundays, after church. She was inflexible on that issue.

Her parents had hired a private coach called Margrit Schmidt who worked at the rink. From a German background, her 'Velvet glove, iron fist' approach, gently but firmly got the best out of each child. Clara's award-winning performances were testament to this at every level. The children were very fond of Margrit. She had a great sense of humour, which she skilfully used to take the bite out of any critique.

Clara's parents, Rosa and Colin Thompson, had taught their daughter well. They nurtured her innate goodness and encouraged her willingness to help those worse off than her at every opportunity.

She had been training harder than usual for the Callachen Junior Gold Cup which was in its seventeenth year. Applicants came from all over the country to take part. As a result, the ice rink was busier than usual and, true to form, Clara was helping out wherever possible.

It was a Thursday evening at about seven-thirty and the light was just starting to fade. Changing into her tracksuit, she zipped up her hoodie and left the arena. Her usual route home was through the town, but that evening she decided to take a far quicker route through the old park by the duck pond. She had been late leaving, so wanted to get home quickly so that her parents wouldn't worry.

Clara loved the duck pond. As usual, people were milling around. It didn't make any difference what time it was. There were always dog walkers, joggers and groups of people chatting and just enjoying being outside.

She hurried through the park to the end of her road and felt relieved that she was nearly home. As she walked along, a familiar, red SUV stopped and the driver called out to her.

She knew him. It was Paul, Margrit's husband, who also worked at the rink as one of the maintenance crew. She loved his black shiny hair that matched his glossy beard and the funny way he laughed and joked about with all the kids at the ice rink.

Over the years, he had taught her snippets about the ice. Clara had a general idea of what good ice and bad ice was. She knew that figure skaters preferred an ice temperature between 26 to 28 F.

She knew this temperature range made the ice softer, which helped grip the edges of the skates. It also stopped the ice from shattering, which would be detrimental to figure skaters.

He had taught her that hockey players needed colder and harder ice conditions. With more players in the rink at the same time, the ice was more likely to shatter, creating a 'crushed ice' effect. The lower temperatures helped to counterbalance the greater activity. She knew all of this because he had befriended her some time ago. And he always talked to her, especially in the Rink Café. He would often tease her about the number of milkshakes she drank.

'Hiya Clara, how are you doing? Margrit asked me to come and see if you could just come back for another half an hour or so. She's desperate. There's some problem with one of the younger kids.'

'Oh, okay. I'll just go and ask my Mum.' replied Clara, glad to be of help.

'Oh don't bother your Mum again. Margrit has already asked her and she said it was okay. Come on, jump in and I'll run you back now.' He smiled encouragingly, gesturing her into the car with a welcoming motion.

Clara recalled the numerous lectures and lessons on 'Stranger Danger', which stressed that a child should never, ever get into a car with a stranger. But Clara instantly put those warnings aside.

It was Paul. She knew Paul. Therefore, he wasn't a stranger, so no danger. Equally, Clara was eager to help someone in need. These two factors caused her to make the worst decision of her life.

'I bet you're thirsty, aren't you? Here, I've brought you one of those milkshakes from the Rink Café. Help yourself.' smiled Paul, as he passed it to her.

'Oh, thank you! I am really, really thirsty.' She smiled her appreciation, as she guzzled the whole contents of the already opened bottle of milkshake.

Chapter

14

Mark Walsh had been liaising with the CEOP (Child Exploitation and Online Protection) Team. He had discovered several instances of internet activity that seemed to correlate with cases the Galaxy team was currently investigating.

During a conversation with an officer called Will, the operator reported that there was increasing online chatter about a previously unknown paedophile network that had been using an echo chamber within a social media platform. The purpose of this was to snare children by targeting specific age groups online. He had worked out that the paedophile network had been able to do this using a rainbow table to intercept the passwords and hash keys of thousands of young people's accounts.

Mark's previous experience with the online vigilante group systems had taught him plenty about who he considered the scum of all humanity. It made his skin crawl when he thought of how the perpetrators worked their way into the hearts and minds of children.

Without a doubt, Mark loved his job and, although he hid it well, he secretly held a torch for Rocco. He was continually trying to earn her respect as a top investigator and desperately hoped that, someday, she would reciprocate the deep feelings he held for her. He often found himself staring at her from behind his computer console. He loved the way she played with her long dark hair, weaving it through her fingers, making loose knots out of a few strands and then letting them fall. She usually did this while she was concentrating as she talked on the telephone. It always made him smile.

Rocco didn't want a relationship with anyone, as she had lost faith in the sanctity of marriage and had become completely disillusioned with love. Her love and care never seemed to be reciprocated with the same intensity and she had found herself always having to fight for more. When she and Trenchie had begun their affair, for a while her mind raced and her heart sang. Trenchie was attractive and treated her like a goddess.

But Rocco was restless and easily bored. For now, she just wanted to be with her family, her siblings and Albie. Her ex-husband Mike would always be a part of that, as he was Albie's father. But her job was her real love and, in that, she was extremely driven.

Her parents love for each other had been unshakeable. She believed that every relationship should be like that. Her expectations had been set so high that they'd become unachievable in every romantic relationship she had been in.

The others in the unit were well aware of Mark's unspoken love for Rocco. Its energy radiated through the office, as an inexhaustible force. Maggie and Stacey took note of every lingering look or smile. If the team ate out or even went for a drink after a particularly gruelling shift, either Maggie or Stacey would manipulate the seating so that Rocco and Mark were forced to sit together. They found it entertaining that Rocco was completely oblivious to his intense feelings for her.

If Mark could crack this case, find the lead that they so badly needed, then maybe, just maybe, she would notice his expertise and him. Rocco was always nice to him, but no more than she was to the rest of the team. She rarely came down with any force on those she managed. However, if anyone was deemed to be not pulling their weight, she was quick to pull them up. Fortunately, such instances were rare indeed.

Mark had hit on a new kind of echo chamber. Using the skills that he had gained over the years for accessing the dark web, he'd found a link to a proposed child auction. It was sickening to read, but he could see that it was imminent.

The epistemic bubble found within the echo chamber was structured so that all of those involved had the same thought processes and sexual attraction to children. He believed it to be similar to a cult, a form of internet brainwashing. Usually echo chambers were more likely to promote set political views while isolating and condemning contradictory views or opinions. However, this one seemed to be more like social interaction, full of codes and systems between paedophile group members, rather than being targeted at or involving children directly. It appeared to be more like a group of like-minded perpetrators, so to speak, to plan and connect.

After nine hours of methodical searching, Mark hit on a lead which linked to something called an 'Access Auction'. He'd found it behind the façade of a craft group on Facebook. He gathered what he needed and took it to the Galaxy Unit office. A briefing was due to be held in the morning and he had a lot of preparation to do for a detailed presentation on what he had found.

This would certainly make her drop her popcorn, he thought to himself, with a smile.

Chapter

15

It was 21:44hrs on Thursday 11th May that another notification came in from the Operations Department about a young girl called Clara Thompson. The stakes were now heightened and Rocco requested more backup for house-to-house enquiries, search teams and a for twenty-four-hour surveillance on each of the families involved. She would need as many Family Liaison Officers as budget and capacity would allow.

Child Rescue Alert

*Missing child
*Clara Thompson
*Braided Afro hair
*Dark brown eyes
*Female – athletic build
*Nine years old

*Last seen leaving the Katrina Ice Rink at approximately 19:35hrs, Thursday.

Rocco was beside herself but was trying to keep it together and maintain her professionalism. She felt such a huge weight of responsibility. Knowing that she would have to face every family member wasn't going to be easy.

Maggie came into her office with a cup of coffee and a homemade brownie. Savouring the chocolate delight, she scoured the missing children paperwork that they had received so far. She kept looking at it to see if there was anything she might have missed, however tenuous the link.

'I'm completely at a loss Mags. We are definitely missing something obvious here. I need to go out for a moment to clear my head.'

'We'll find a link, Roc. We always do. Just keep doing what you're doing. I did think that it might be a good idea to set up a group for the parents and family of those missing children, seeing as how there are so many. And God forbid, who knows if there will be even more? I'll try and get two more Family Liaison Officers seconded to our Unit to make four of them.' replied Maggie, in her usual efficient manner as she left her boss's office.

Rocco was exhausted. She hadn't slept well for over a week. She was frustrated that she still didn't have anything substantial to go on. She completed the paperwork and distributed it to the team before calling yet another briefing.

The Galaxy Team was working as much as was humanly possible. They each had their tasks and had reported their findings, Rocco made sure they were following protocol to the letter.

'Right. Keep what we've got so far, but let's go back to the beginning. And remember to keep an open mind.' said Rocco.

The first three hours were critically important in any missing child case. They were often referred to as the Golden Hours. Within this timeframe, every available resource was used when a child was reported missing. It was seen as the critical window of opportunity because of the vulnerability of the child. Therefore, as more and more children were disappearing, it came as no surprise that Rocco got the resources she needed. She set up a dedicated central telephone number. It ensured that all calls were answered only by a member of the Galaxy Unit so that nothing would be missed, ignored or lost.

The information was being cross-checked against specific criteria and then quickly passed to the senior officers on the case. There wasn't a second to lose.

Chapter

16

As Stacey Lord walked Anthony Jerome through to the interview room, she nodded to her boss as she passed the corridor where she was deep in a conversation with Hesh.

Rocco was hot on their tail, as this one and only witness was taken through his paces in the interview room.

Police Interview

Witness Account- Anthony Jerome

Present: DCI Rochelle Raven, PC Mahesh Cole, Mr Anthony Jerome.

'Mr Jerome, thank you for coming in to make this witness statement. Can you start by telling us exactly what you saw.' asked Hesh.

'Well, I was just on my way back from the school run. I could see this old couple talking to a little boy from their car window and then they got out to talk to him, you know, like kneeling down to his height, sort of thing.' replied a very nervous Anthony Jerome.

'Can you remember the colour and make of the car, Mr Jerome?' Hesh continued.

'No idea of the make but the car was definitely silver.'

'What do you remember about the old couple?' asked Hesh.

'Well, they were both quite fit and pretty tall, she especially, and unusually so for their age, I thought. They seemed to be umm, what's the right word? Enticing. Yes, that's it. They were enticing him by showing him a puppy. I can't believe people still use that old chestnut!'

'So Mr Jerome, is it fair to say then, that in your opinion, the child was not actually with the elderly couple?' asked Rocco.

'Yes, I think it's fair to say that. Definitely. It was only afterwards that I really thought about it. When it was in the paper. And then it became obvious that children have been going missing from the news reports and all that!'

'Would you recognise either of the elderly couple if you saw them again, Mr Jerome? What I mean by that is that we have a forensic sketch artist who will take the basic details from your description and then create a digital version. But, this would require you to come back into the station. Would you be okay with that?' asked Rocco.

'I think so yes. I'd be prepared to give it a go, anyway.'

'Okay, thank you, Mr Jerome. That's all we need for today unless you can remember anything else about that day? If anything else comes up for you, please give me or my colleague a call. My sergeant here will see you out and thanks again for your time. You have been really helpful.'

Anthony Jerome left the interview room escorted by Hesh. They walked through the police station and out to Anthony's car.

'I hope I've helped in some small way.' offered Anthony.

'You have indeed, Mr Jerome. I'm sure you have.' said Hesh, reassuringly.

When he returned, Rocco was looking unsettled. She had reservations about the man they had just interviewed.

'Have him followed, Hesh. I want twenty-four-hour surveillance on him for the next seven days. If he's got anything to do with that little lad's disappearance he will lead us to him. In between that, we need to arrange the forensic sketch artist as soon as possible. He is our one and only lead at the moment.' ordered Rocco.

Chapter

17

The office was buzzing. While most of the team were out investigating the sudden rise in missing children, the phones were ringing constantly. The missing children's parents, as well as the Galaxy Team, were on high alert. Stress levels were through the roof, exacerbated by continuous interference from the media.

'It's for you, Rocco. Sounds a bit more urgent than usual, Ma'am.' called Hesh, as he put the call through.

'Transfer it to my office. Thanks, Hesh.' called Rocco. DCI Raven closed the door as she picked up the call. It was Mike, her ex-husband.

'Why didn't you let me know that Albie was with you? We normally keep each other updated, Rocco.'

'Mike, I don't know what you're talking about. Of course, I always let you know. If he's not with you, and he's not with me, then where the fuck is he?' demanded the chief inspector.

'I'll check with Conrad and Niamh. Maybe one of them has taken him for a burger.' she offered.

'I've already contacted them. They both said he must be with you. Albie knows the rules. He knows to keep one of us updated with his whereabouts. That's how this whole living at both houses works.' replied Mike, clearly irritated.

'Look, just keep ringing his friends' houses and I'll pass this through as a missing child right now. When did you last see him?' asked Rocco, desperately trying to stay calm.

'This morning. I dropped him off at school and when I went to collect him from the after- school swimming club, he wasn't there. Come over later, will you? We need to be clear about where we go from here.' Mike hesitated a moment before adding 'Isn't this a bit melodramatic, Rocco? Missing child. I mean, what's going on?'

'Mike, we have children going missing left, right and centre here. I can't tell you any more than that at the moment. Two of my officers will be with you within the hour to take a statement. There must be CCTV at the sports centre. There must be something, at least one clue! He can't have vanished into thin air!'

Rocco felt dizzy and her blood ran cold. She rushed to the ladies' room, where she was violently sick. Somewhere deep within her, she knew he had been taken. She just knew.

'Are you alright, Ma'am?' whispered Stacey, who had followed Rocco into the bathroom.

'They've taken my boy, Stacey! I just know it.' cried Rocco as she fell to her knees.

Sergeant Stacey Lord gave her a minute, then gently helped her to a chair. She was a straight-talking but empathic officer and told her boss the truth about the situation.

'Look, Ma'am. I know this is difficult if that really is the case that Albie has been taken. I've got two kids myself. I cannot imagine what you are going to go through in the next few hours or however long it takes to find him. But you are going to be of no bloody use to him if you fall apart. You've got to get a grip and do what you do best. You have all of us behind you, and we will find him, I promise you that. We will find him.'

Rocco took a deep breath, walked over to the basin, and splashed her face with cold water.

'You're right, I've got to do this properly, and try, somehow, to take the emotion out of it or the Super will take me off the case. And I can't have that. I can't let someone else find him, can I?' stated Rocco, desperation in her voice.

'Now look. You stay here for a minute while I'll go and get your bag. You can sort your makeup out, and get back in there.' said Stacey, in her usual straight- to- the- point style.

Maggie, who had been sent by Stacey, came into the ladies' room and immediately put her arms around Rocco in a motherly gesture.

'Come on, honey. Let's get you sorted and back in the office.'

Mike came into the station after the police had been to take a statement. He didn't understand why there was such panic. Albie had gone AWOL before, but he was always just out with his mates or playing football somewhere. But now, he was panicking too and he and Rocco went into her office and closed the door. She couldn't go into detail but gave him an overview of the situation and what she believed might have happened.

'Is it because he's your son, do you think? Has someone got it in for you?' asked Mike, unable to look her in the eyes.

It was no secret that he hated her job and everything that came with it. In his mind, it had robbed him of his wife and contributed to his son having an absent mother.

'No, I definitely think it's a coincidence. But even so, we've got to be sure. We've got to check all of his mates' houses first. Then arcades, parks. You know what he's like. We need to look everywhere and anywhere he could have gone. I'm so hoping I've got this wrong.'

They left the office together. On reaching the car park, they decided to split up. They got into separate cars to go to each and every one of Albie's friends' houses. Conrad was calling on the car phone just as Rocco started to drive away and she clicked the answer button on the steering wheel.

'Hey, Sis. How's it going, did Mike find Albie?' asked her brother, happily.

'Not good, Con. Not good at all. We can't find him and I'm so scared that he's been taken by someone. We have several children of his age who have gone missing recently and I am so, so scared Con.'

'Whoa! Hold on! What do you mean 'missing'? Where are you now?' asked Conrad, with a sudden sense of urgency.

'Mike and I are visiting his mates' houses. The team here are checking his school premises. I've allocated another team to go door-to-door within a ten-mile radius from his school.' replied Rocco, her work head kicking back in.

'I'm on my way, Sis. I'll call the others. We'll be back at yours in case he comes home, okay?' reassured Conrad.

Rocco ended the call by clicking the OFF symbol on the steering wheel. She made her way to the first of Albie's friends on her list.

Chapter

18

Clara Thompson was usually a dreamy, happy child, with great aims and aspirations for her future. Her parents were demonstrably proud of her dedication to the sport she loved and everything she had achieved in her young life.

Right now, though, she was dizzy and disorientated. She had no idea where she was or how she had gotten there.

She had the very best of everything, and her parents and grandparents, who lived with them, ensured a safe and nurturing environment for her. She had never known squalor or violence or, indeed, anything that might be considered unclean or questionable.

Her bedroom had been painted a warm white, the walls adorned with her many ice skating rosettes. The shelves were buckling with yet more trophies, her victories in the junior championships.

Closing her eyes, she tried to focus on positive thoughts and memories.

How she had been told that she had made the triple axels look easy. Triple axels were a particularly challenging jump formation. It had been Margrit's encouragement, insistence and firm coaching that had given Clara the confidence and courage to master all but two of the six main jumps required in championship routines.

She reminded herself how, in her last competition, she had launched herself from the outside edge of one skate, rotated in the air, and landed on the outer side of the opposite skate. She had done it perfectly, a triple axel with no flaws. Three perfect turns before she landed as softly as a butterfly.

Clara had incredible body strength. Her young frame was so finely honed from all of the training, effort and time that she invested in herself and her sport. That strength and determination was exactly what she needed to be successful, to get to the right height and speed to complete the turns before landing firmly on the ice. That was when she was truly in her element.

Opening her eyes, she looked around the room. There was just a sliver of light from a crack in the window board. She knew that she was in trouble. Her hands were cut and her body felt bruised and sore, quite different from the usual aches and pains after training. Flashes of memories fired within her tired brain. Was it her friend Paul who she'd seen last? Didn't he give her a lift home? Where was her mum, dad and Duke, her grandfather? Where were Grandma and Flute, their Golden Labrador?

Clara started to cry at the sound of thundering footsteps overhead. She heard a key in the lock and the light stung her eyes as a tall, strange old man stood in front of her, smiling. 'Hello, my dear. My name is Lance.'

Chapter

19

Mike had made the 'missing child' call to the police so that it was recorded, just as his ex-wife had asked him to. Rocco already had all resources on it anyway, but it needed it to be made formal, without her involvement, so that she wouldn't be taken off the case.

Child Rescue Alert

*Missing child
*Albie Raven
*Dark Blonde Hair
*Emerald Green Eyes
*Male – tall for his age
*Eight years old
*Last seen by the receptionist at the Leisure Centre.

The official notification came through. Rocco rushed out to the ladies room where, again, she was physically sick.

Stacey followed a few minutes later, carrying a drink of water and a sweet biscuit. She didn't say anything. She let her boss pull herself together, in her own time. There was no need for words.

They both knew that it was action that was needed now. Rocco could feel her maternal instincts welling up in her body. She felt like a tiger on a leash. She was going to find those bastards, even if it was with her last breath.

Chapter

20

The investigation into the disappearance of more and more children was now called Operation Saturn and it was gathering momentum.

Nationwide searches had begun within forty-eight hours of each child's disappearance. Press releases had been presented twice by Rocco and Edward Trenchard. The nation was on high alert, following the announcement that a serial child abductor was on the loose. Every newspaper headline presented a different scenario. Well-wishers from all over the world sent their love and support. It was making the front pages of Broadsheets across the world. One highly respected British newspaper led with the following story:

"Police are searching for five missing eight to nine-year-olds who, they suspect, have been abducted by the same person or persons"

Rochelle Raven stated that the Galaxy Unit of the Callachen Police was becoming increasingly concerned for the missing children's safety and has deployed a large number of officers and specialist teams to investigate the disappearances.

Hundreds of local residents in the towns of Callachen Reaches and Callachen All Saints were offering to help, including offers to join search parties.

Detective Chief Inspector Rochelle Raven and Detective Chief Superintendent Edward Trenchard stated that police were following several lines of inquiry. DCSI Trenchard stated that Callachen Police, together with neighbouring forces, had launched an intensive search and criminal investigation into the abduction of the missing children. The communities of the neighbouring towns were shocked by these events. People found it incredulous that such a thing could happen in their supposedly, safe and protected neighbourhoods and communities.

Police released pictures of the children, urging anyone with information to come forward.

A representative from each family continued to liaise with the Galaxy team, helping with background information for the press including online, television, radio and newspapers.

An unprecedented number of four FLOs had been assigned to work with the affected families. An informal meeting point and office had been set up in the spare lounge of Holley Knowles mother's house.

All of the parents were regularly visited by their allocated FLO. They could also attend the group, either to provide information or support or just to sit in silence, whatever was needed.

The Galaxy team had moved quickly after each child had been reported missing. Rocco had requested further backup and support for the house to house enquiries. The search of cars, lorries and old buildings was extended. Extra analysis teams and continued surveillance on all of the families involved was critical. It was all the police had to go on at the moment.

Maggie continued the coordination work in the FLO department. She had been instrumental in setting up the support group for the parents being held every Wednesday evening. Every single person was being watched for any suspicious behaviour. FLOs were being rotated among the families. The liaison officers were acutely aware of the role they were expected to play. Gathering evidence to assist in the investigation was their primary emphasis. Most of the parents were aware of their true focus within the families.

Over time, the family support group evolved into a constructive outlet for parental rage and fear, as the parents and guardians became more familiar and comfortable in each other's presence.

As well as the head liaison officer, there was also a spokesperson for the families group. Leon Dalton's mother had stepped forward to keep herself grounded and allow for some psychological order and headspace. It was the only way she knew how to cope.

They each shared their stories. Their pain and angst were palpable but they knew, without doubt, that they needed to stick together, to show strength and to be available for every call, every search and every scrap of information that came in.

It had been hard for everyone to maintain a daily routine, but they needed to do this. The driving force behind each search effort was each one of them. They each had different strengths and weaknesses. But each knew they had to be strong if they had any chance of surviving this horrific ordeal. It was for their children's sakes because the awful truth was that the nightmare would continue until every single child was found.

It was incredibly difficult for all of them, but together, they buoyed each other. Having group meals at Heather Knowles house gave them a sense of togetherness and cohesiveness. If one couldn't sleep, the others would encourage short naps, while they kept watch for news. For some, talking with the others was extremely beneficial as it unleashed an outpouring of emotion that may otherwise have been internalised. Getting outside for walks or other physical activity helped to alleviate the stress.

They took turns going to the park so that there was always someone present in the house, in case of any developments. Being surrounded by others offered a slight distraction from the anguish that tore through their hearts.

As the group bonded, each parent disclosed feelings of self-blame. It was a roller-coaster ride of how there must have been something that they could or might have done to prevent their child from disappearing without a trace. If they hadn't had each other, this group, this setting, they would have driven themselves crazy with the 'what ifs' and 'whys'.

Sophie Dalton encouraged others to take as many breaks as possible. Clara's parents made an endless supply of food for everyone. They knew that to keep strong and to endure what was or what might be to come, they all needed food and sleep. Nothing else mattered, except keeping well and ready for welcoming their children home. No one dared speak the unspeakable.

Chapter

21

Clara Thompson- Parents' Interview

Present: DCI Rochelle Raven, PC Mahesh Cole, Mr Colin Thompson, Mrs Rosa Thompson.

'Thank you for coming in to talk to us, Mr and Mrs Thompson. We will try to make this as painless as possible. I want you to know that we are doing absolutely everything we can to find your daughter. We just need to ask a few questions to ensure that we haven't missed anything. Is that okay? We will both be asking you about the events leading up to Clara's disappearance to help us with finding Clara.' stated Rocco, as she led the meeting.

'Thank you.' answered Rosa.

'So Mrs Thompson, can you tell us the last time you saw Clara?' asked Hesh.

'She left for school and went straight to the ice rink for her training, same as she does every evening after school. I checked with Margrit when she didn't come home.' replied Rosa.

'I'm sorry Mr and Mrs Thompson, but not knowing where your child is or how she is being treated is one of the hardest things a parent will have to endure.' said Rocco, thinking of her own sweet boy.

'Thank you. Both of us are finding it really difficult to understand what has happened to our beautiful daughter. She is such a good girl, so helpful and trusting and would help anyone in trouble.' added Colin.

'We have witnesses who saw your daughter walking through the duck pond park at approximately 19:50 hrs on the day that she went missing. What we don't understand is how on earth she could have just vanished in that short space of time between the duck pond park and your house?' queried Hesh.

'She had been training harder than usual, really pushing herself for the Ice Skating Juniors Gold Cup, but she always helps out there, with the little ones, you know. She's never any trouble' continued her father.

'Can I ask if either of you have any idea why Clara may have come home through the duck pond park instead of through the town, how she usually came.' asked Hesh.

'Clara loved being around the duck pond. I used to take her there when she was a toddler. It was such a safe place for her and it would have been quicker for her to come home that way.' answered her mother.

'I know this is difficult for you Mrs Thompson but we just need to ask a few more questions, to get a sense of Clara and what she may have been doing when she went missing. Is that okay?' continued Rocco.

Rosa Thompson was very distressed and her husband interrupted, with a question of his own.

'Do you have any leads at all? As parents, we are trying so hard to stay positive.'

'I'm sorry, but we can't discuss that Mr Thompson. Let's stick with the information you have about your daughter. What are her likes and dislikes? Does she use social media at all?' enquired Hesh.

'We are very careful about what we allow Clara to watch and get involved in. If anything, she is a bit sheltered from what you would consider a modern streetwise, child. Maybe it's our fault for being too protective.' replied Rosa.

'It's always been our way, you know, to keep her safe. She must have been taken because she may well be sheltered but she's also a very sensible girl.' said Colin, coming to his daughter's defence.

'We will do our very best to find your daughter and get her back home to you. If, in the meantime, you think of anything else that might help us with our enquiries, please contact us immediately and we will get straight back to you.' replied Hesh.

'Okay. Thank you, Mr and Mrs Thompson. That will be all we need for today, and as my colleague here has just said if you can remember anything else about that day, or if anything else comes up, please do not hesitate to call us. PC Hesh will see you out and thanks again for your time.' said Rocco.

The Thompsons were escorted out to their car. Mrs Thompson was barely able to function behind the cascade of tears that had begun to fall. The interview with the police had made it real. Clara really was missing.

Hesh waved them off and walked back into the station. He was so tired. It was all getting too much, seeing such raw pain. Noticing Rocco in the kitchen, he asked if he could go home and get a couple of hours sleep.

Rocco looked at him, nodded and went out into the main office and asked who wanted to have a night off to get some rest and be back by the early hours. She knew how important it was to keep the team's morale up, if she was going to get the best out of them.

There was some slight hesitation before the whole team, including Maggie, gathered their belongings and got ready to leave the office.

'What about you Rocco? What will you do?' asked Maggie.

'Well, I have a meeting with the chief before I can do anything. But once that's over I'll probably head home too. We'll all be more effective if we have clear heads. We're missing something, I just know we are. Sometimes a little time alone to think about a case is worth more than trawling through all the evidence in front of you over and over again.' replied Rocco.

Chapter

22

Albie, who was tall and muscular for his age, felt sick to his stomach. He could never have imagined feeling and seeing such horror, with men and women looking at his body, touching him through his clothing and stroking his face. As their fingers caressed the contours of his small lips, he couldn't help but cringe at the strange looks on their faces as they did. He had been taught never to let anybody, not anybody, touch his body without his consent and until now, no one, not ever, had.

His body had gone rigid. He was in shock. He knew this was wrong, so wrong. His mind was in chaos. He couldn't move his limbs. He felt frozen. His eyes, the only part of his body that he seemed to be able to move, scanned the room as if to distance himself from what was happening.

He saw the bookshelves that lined the high walls of the old room. They were full of, what appeared to be, leather-bound books. He'd never seen so many in one place, except maybe, at the old school library.

He noticed two high ladders on wheels that must have been used for reaching the books along the higher shelves. His attention was drawn back to the room as three more children were brought into the big room. There were two boys, one quite tiny with dark blonde hair and one wearing green glasses and a girl with lots of freckles and pretty white-blonde hair, all about the same age as himself.

These latest arrivals had been brought in by a tall and glamourous elderly woman, whose name he'd overheard was Gloria. He recognised her instantly as the woman at the swimming pool and also from his school where she had visited before, for something to do with welfare. As she presented the children in a line-up, the other adults seemed to get very excited, moving in their seats and nudging each other. Gloria stood up to speak.

'Hello everyone. I hope you are enjoying this preliminary viewing and have got your initial bids in order. The Full Access Auction will be taking place in the next few weeks. The time and date will be given in the usual way, on the web. Following a successful bid, you will be able to take your purchase home with you. I hope you have a good day. Please help yourself to refreshments, which will be served in the next hour. Do not touch the merchandise, if you can help yourselves.' Gloria smiled.

Albie was told to stand with the others and, one by one, they were called forward. He was shocked to realise that the adults were actually bidding for children. Just like the boat auctions at the harbour his dad took him to on Saturday mornings during the school holidays. He couldn't understand. Maybe they weren't able to have children and he and the others were being sold and maybe he would be taken to another country to be a child to new parents.

Albie started to sob quietly. No way! He didn't want new parents. He wanted his own mum and dad. He wanted Uncle Conrad, Martin and Auntie Niamh. He wanted his room at the mill and at his dad's house. He wanted his friends. He just wanted to go home.

A tall man called Frankie with ginger hair and a beard won him with the highest bid of what he thought he heard as sixty thousand pounds. He was taken to the back of the room and told not to move. Suddenly, profound fear surged through his body. Albie continued to watch as the other three children were also auctioned off and then told to stand in line with him at the back of the room.

When the auction was over, a teenage girl was called in. He noticed that she had something wrong with her mouth and her lip. He knew it was called a hare lip or something like that because he'd seen the advert on TV where people could donate money to help African children smile again.

He remembered how, on asking his uncle Conrad if he was old enough to help them, Conrad had told him that he would set up a standing order to send a regular amount each month in Albie's name to the charity if that's what he wanted. Together, they had worked to sell his old toys, books, Xbox game sets and other bits and pieces so he could raise enough money to help these little children. He wondered why this girl, this teenager, had not had the chance to have the operation when she was younger. Focusing on this, seemed to take his mind away from the horror that was taking place right before his eyes.

Annie was ordered to take the children away, to be fed and washed so that they would be kept clean and healthy for their new owners. As he left with the other children, he could see the adults handing over large bundles of cash to the man and woman. He'd recognised them as the ones who had taken him from the sports centre as he waited for his Dad to collect him after swimming.

He recalled that he'd been in the foyer. He had been desperate for a drink after his swimming lesson. The drinks machine hadn't been working, so he had gone to the receptionist to ask for some water. An elderly woman, who he now knew as Gloria, was waiting in the queue. Upon hearing his request she'd offered him a drink. She'd said that she had a crate of Coca Cola leftover from her son's party. He was welcome to one if he didn't mind coming to the car, as her old legs wouldn't let her walk so far and back these days.

She had reminded him of his late grandma, and without any thought of danger, Albie followed the kind elderly woman to her car.

As he leaned in to reach for a can of coke, he was suddenly hit over the head with a hard, heavy object. Albie slumped into the back seat of the car. The elderly couple drove out of the sports centre car park, at the exact moment that his dad turned in to the centre to collect him.

'What's going on? Are they going to hurt us?' Albie whispered to Annie.

'I'm not supposed to talk to you, but I'm not going to lie to you either. They hurt everyone. Yes, they are going to hurt you, like you could never imagine. But I have drugs that will help. I save them for all the children. If you're lucky, nothing will happen until you leave with one of the buyers.' whispered Annie.

Albie looked at her in terror. He was completely frozen with dread. Annie kept the four children moving. When they got to the huge bathroom, she ran a bath and choose clothes for each of them from a large box by the door. She poured strawberry scented bubble bath into the water and gave each of them a small bar of soap. She informed them that they would have to bathe every day until instructed otherwise.

'Can't you help us, Annie? There's still time, isn't there?' pleaded Albie, his eyes boring into her.

'I might be able to. I've been thinking about it for a while. But don't ask me again, okay.'

Chapter

23

Niamh had arrived minutes before Conrad and Martin. They busied themselves cleaning. No one dared mention the state their sister had left the kitchen. She was usually meticulously tidy.

Rocco arrived home even later than usual, having given the rest of her team the night off. Her family couldn't help but notice the exhaustion etched on her face. They took turns hugging her as they cried together.

'So look, Sis. We're all going to stay awhile, okay. Just so that you get some decent food. You need all your strength right now and we can be here at the mill in case Albie comes home.' said Conrad.

'Thanks, guys. That means so much. I don't think I can be on my own right now. I'm so tired but I keep thinking about Albie. If he is okay, if he is being hurt or, the very worst, if he is already dead.' Rocco sobbed as she collapsed onto the hard stone floor.

Niamh got down on the floor with her sister. 'Now listen to me. He will be okay, Roc. He is a strong boy. He and his dad go camping and walking all the time. Do you remember that time when Mike left him in the Lake District and told him to find his way back to the lodge? He got back with no trouble. He camped out that night. Remember?'

'Yes, thank goodness Mike was stalking him though. I would have killed Mike if he'd really left him.' Rocco smiled at the memory.

'He will be okay, Sis. I just know he will. Whoever's got him has picked the wrong kid. You wait and see!' Conrad chipped in to console his sister.

The doorbell chimed and Martin went to answer it.

'Do you mind if I stay here for a while?' Mike asked, was in tears as he came into the room.

'Of course you can, Mike. Come here. Let's go and talk for a while.' replied Rocco, leading him into the sitting room, where there was a beautiful log fire burning.

Niamh brought in two glasses of red wine. 'Dinner won't be long, guys.'

Neither Rocco nor Mike had the heart to tell her that they weren't hungry. It turned out that they didn't have to.

'I know what you're thinking. But you both have to stay strong for Albie.' smiled Niamh, as she went back into the kitchen.

Chapter

24

Paddy Ward was the youngest of six children from a strong, line of Irish Travellers. His mother, Rosalie, and father, who was also called Patrick, had moved into one of the permanent settlements provided by the council.

The local authorities had a responsibility to provide housing for the travelling population. As part of the local planning framework, the council addressed housing needs for all families who passed the assessment for the provision of different types of accommodation, taking into account people's different ways of life.

Paddy had been hanging around with the usual kids at the park. He had been showing them how to heal a cut with the direct flame from his lighter. It was a long tradition in his family. The other children were in awe of him. Paddy had a pony too, a piebald called Gentle Herod. He told tales of his antics at the Appleby Horse Fair, where he and his family went every year.

How they would ride their horses through the water and have such a great time. It was what he looked forward to for the whole year.

Sometimes he would ride his beloved horse to the park. He was a hero as far as the other kids were concerned. So daring and cheeky, especially with the girls.

Most of the children at the park followed the tacit street laws of their community which had been handed down for generations. One such rule dictated that children had to be indoors once the street lights were switched on. Life was different for Paddy. He didn't have to be in at any particular time.

It was on one such evening, long after the street lights had come on, that Paddy was walking Gentle Herod back to his field. A car stopped just ahead. He saw the lights go out and he noticed that the driver had stayed put.

Pretending that he hadn't seen it, he continued chattering to his horse. As he walked passed the car, he thought he recognised the driver as the man who worked at the ice rink. He thought his name was Paul. He had seen him in the café. As the man beckoned to the boy, Paddy noticed that the man seemed to be in some kind of trouble. His face was distorted and he was holding his hand across his chest.

The hazard lights were on. Paddy saw the car window slide down as the man called out to him. 'Hey, lad. Hey, can you help me? I think I need an ambulance!'

Paddy tied the horse lead to a post and ran across to the man. Leaning halfway into the car window, the boy said 'Hiya. You alright, mate?'

'Can you just jump in here quickly and make a phone call on my mobile. I don't want to die on my own. I'm scared and I think I'm having some kind of a heart attack.' The man's face was still screwed up. He was squirming and breathing heavily.

Paddy's grandad had recently had a heart attack and it was he who had found him and called for the ambulance. By now, Paddy was certain that he recognised the man. The man's face continued to look contorted and Paddy thought he was going to die. Wanting to help the man, just like he did with everyone, concern overrode his survival instinct. He opened the car door and climbed in.

As Paddy got into the car, the man pointed to the glove box. Between gasps, he asked the boy to get his mobile charger out. As Paddy reached for the handle, he felt a stabbing pain as the needle was plunged into his neck.

Within seconds, the boy was drifting into unconsciousness, thanks to the GHB, liquid ecstasy, now flowing into his bloodstream.

One sneaky glance around, then Paul quickly drove off towards the Magpie House. Wow! He was going to make a killing on this one! Oh yes, indeed! The upcoming auction was well on its way to being the best one ever.

Chapter

25

<u>Witness Interview-Margrit Schmidt Horton</u>

Present: DCI Rochelle Raven, Sergeant Stacey Lord, Mrs Margrit Schmidt-Horton.

'Thank you, Margrit for coming in today to tell us about Clara. We will try and be as quick as we can.' said Rocco.

'That's okay. I am very worried about Clara. She is my best student. Continually winning awards for our club.'

'Thank you. What else can you tell us about Clara?' asked Stacey.

'Well, just what a helpful, well-adjusted child she is. I rely on her quite a bit to help with the young ones, to be honest. She says she doesn't mind and that she enjoys helping. Oh my, I just hope she is okay.'

'When did you last see Clara Thompson, Margrit?' quizzed Rocco.

'She left at about seven-thirty, or thereabouts. She waved to me as she left, with her usual beautiful smile.'

'Was there anything unusual or different about her on that evening or during her time at the ice rink?' asked Stacey.

'No, nothing. She was her normal happy and bubbly self. I have racked my brain to think if there's anything I've missed. You know, boys or new friends, but she didn't seem any different at all.'

'Do you remember if she spoke to anyone else before she left?' asked Rocco, alternating with Stacy, as they had previously agreed.

'Well, probably the girls in the café and my husband, Paul. They usually have some banter. He is friends with all the kids, boys and girls and their parents.' replied Margrit.

'That's fine Margrit. Of course, we will be interviewing him later today. In the meantime, if you think of anything at all that might help, we'd be grateful if you could give us a call.'

The interview ended, with Rocco and Stacey being no further forward. Maybe the husband would tell them more later, Rocco thought.

Chapter

26

It was 08:24hrs on Saturday, 18th May that another emergency notification came in from the operations department. This time it concerned a young traveller boy named Patrick Ward. Rocco was exhausted as she read the details to Maggie and Stacey, who were both in her office. The details jumped out at her and she seemed transfixed by every single word.

Child Rescue Alert

*Missing child
*Patrick Ward
*Auburn hair
*Pale freckly skin
*Bright blue eyes
*Male – small build
*Nine years old
*Last seen leaving the park

This was just getting ridiculous! What was happening? She was at a loss as to what to do next. She cradled her head in her hands as she fell back into her chair.

Suddenly, she stood up and left the office with her 'emergency' pack of cigarettes. Heading out to the grassed area behind the office, she was spotted by DCSI Trenchard, who immediately followed her.

'Why are you smoking again? 'What's wrong?'

'Trench, this is going far too fast for us. This is a serial child snatcher or it's trafficking at a scale that we've never seen or known before. I'm at a loss. I'm exhausted and I don't know what to do. I don't want you to take me off the case because of Albie.'

'Listen, Roc. I've been watching all of you and keeping up to date with everything you've been doing with this investigation. Not to mention what you must be going through with Albie being taken as well. Will it help if I intervene, if I call a briefing and head it up? Will you feel backed up?'

'You know what Trench that would be excellent. It'll help me to see it from the back of the room, rather than the front. We can establish everything we've already got and work with separating the team more. Thank you so much for this.'

Trenchie nodded. 'Okay Roc, get the briefing set up for midday today. Warn everybody that we may be there for a few hours. We need to set everyone robust tasks to be actioned today and possibly this evening. We've got to try and utilise everything in our power to prevent any more children going missing.'

Rocco walked back into her office and quickly reached for some mints from her desk drawer.

'I don't know why you think that will help. We can still smell it, you know.' smiled Maggie, trying to lighten the mood a little.

Rocco returned the smile. She asked Maggie to prep the briefing room and round up the team including all of the external officers working on each of the missing children cases. Maggie was also tasked to contact the safeguarding team at the council and to collate any information they had so that it could be presented at the briefing.

'We need every bit of CCTV footage that we have obtained so far of each child's movements, weeks before they went missing or even the day before. All their last movements. I want you to cancel any pending leave for the foreseeable future. We need everyone on this. We need food and refreshments for 15:00hrs we are in for a long afternoon and evening, Maggie.'

Chapter

27

Holly knew that there was something different about tonight. Annie had her chores to do, one of which was to go down to that awful pit and feed young Holly. Annie told her that the plan was that in a few weeks, she would be washed, dressed and taken up to the big room for the big auction. Some very important men and women were coming to see her.

After the preliminary auction that had taken place, her purchase would be confirmed and she would be collected and taken away.

Annie looked at Holly and shushed. 'Don't speak. Just listen to me. This is your only chance to get out of here. Do it tonight. Wait until after midnight. They are both usually drunk and asleep by then. I'll leave the door unlocked. When you get up there, follow the hall down to the end, and then turn right. There's a side door. I'll leave that unlocked, as well.'

Holly looked at Annie in amazement. Annie had stashed a pile of clothes and a pair of trainers by the wall. Holly could barely make them out, having just the light from the crack in the door.

'What about you? Will you run, too?' whispered Holly, wide-eyed.

Annie shook her head. 'No, I can't. I will be missed. Look, kid. If you do get away, if you find help, there's just one thing I need you to do for me. I saw a policewoman on the telly when I was cleaning in the drawing-room. I need you to get this letter to her. She's the one with long black hair. I think her name is Raven or something like that.' Annie pushed the folded letter into the front pocket of the jeans that she had found for the girl.

Holly nodded to her rescuer. Her thoughts raced as she tried to work out how she could get away with this, how she could get people to come back and rescue her friend. What if she got caught? What if they have dogs? She couldn't recall hearing any dogs. Her mind continued to race. What if? What if? What if?

Shaken out of her trance, Holly felt Annie's hands on her shoulders. 'Now, focus. You have got to get away. You are all there is, all that can save any of us now. You are the only chance we have.' Annie looked straight into the child's eyes, a combination of hope and dread in her voice.

'Okay, Annie. I'll try.'

Annie cut the tie wrap from Holly's wrist and helped her to get dressed into the clothes she had ready for her. As Annie climbed the stairs back to whatever hell awaited her, she turned and waved.

She hoped to God and all the angels that Lance Mountford wouldn't choose this night to visit Holly.

Chapter

28

Paddler's Walk was the new estate built to accommodate ex-travelling communities. It was open to anyone who had decided to end their caravanning days and settle permanently. It was located on the outskirts of Callachen Town. Stacey and Mark didn't like to go there at all.

As they arrived at Mr and Mrs Ward's home, they were greeted by the sound of barking dogs. Barking dogs usually meant danger. However, it turned out to be two very friendly Staffordshire bull terriers, which belonged to the Ward family.

'Well, you took your bloody time, didn't you?' challenged a man as he opened the door, wearing the stereotypical string vest while shushing the dogs away.

'Oh, hello. You must be Mr Ward. I'm PC Mark Walsh and this is Sergeant Stacey Lord. We're here to take a few details regarding the disappearance of your son. May we come in?'

'Let them in, Paddy. And don't be so rude to the lady and gentleman. They are trying to help us, after all.' Mrs Ward appeared with a tray of biscuits and the offer of tea.

'Mrs Ward, can you tell me what happened, please? And do you have a current photo of Patrick that we can take away with us or I could take a copy with my phone?' asked Mark.

'Well, he was here yesterday. He took Herod out for his exercise. It was when one of the other children brought the horse back this morning without little Paddy, that we realised he was gone.' replied Mrs Ward.

'Okay, okay. Do either of you know where he had been or where the horse had been left?' asked Stacey.

'The kid who brought the horse back said it was just left tied up at the park. Gone off with some girlie, no doubt.' Mr Ward smirked, as he answered the question.

Stacey, not liking his cavalier tone, decided to put him straight.

'Mr Ward, are you aware that we have had several children go missing in the last eight weeks. We are extremely concerned that your *nine*-year-old son could be one of those.' Stacey stressed 'nine' to emphasise the total inappropriateness of his comments.

'Ah, I don't think anyone would take our Paddy. He will come home when he's hungry enough, for sure.'

Well, so much for her comment, then.

'Please let us know if he comes back or if you hear anything at all. We must speak to him. In the meantime, we will do our utmost to find him, Mr and Mrs Ward. Thank you for the tea and biscuits.'

Rosalie Ward produced two photographs from an old tin, one of which was of her son with his beloved horse and one of him at the ice rink with his friends from school. She handed them to Stacey, who had requested them earlier.

'Mrs Ward, does Paddy go to the ice rink often?' asked Stacey.

Both Stacey and Mark could feel a surge of excitement.

'Well yes, as a matter of fact. He loves it there. He goes whenever he can, but he is also devoted to his horse. It kind of takes up all of his money, when he has it, that is. That's how I know he is missing because he would never, ever not feed or walk Herod, not for anything or anyone.'

Stacey and Mark left the house and sat in their police car.

'I'm getting a really bad feeling about this ice rink, Mark. Aren't you?'

'Well, it's odd, isn't it? How one of the missing kids was a skater and now this one was a regular visitor.'

'Right. We'd better ring this in. I'll drive and you call it into the office. Let's give that ice rink another visit, shall we?'

Chapter

29

Police Interview

Paul Horton- Personal Account

Present: DCI Rochelle Raven, Sergeant Stacey Lord, Mr Paul Horton.

'So, Paul. May I call you Paul? I understand that you were one of the last people to see young Clara Thompson. Is that correct?' Rocco began the questioning.

'Yes, Paul is fine. Yes, I did see Clara, as I do every day. I waved to her as she left which was about half seven.'

'You didn't see her again, Paul?' asked Stacey, looking straight at him.

'No definitely not. Like I said, I saw her leave and I waved to her, as I always do. What is this? Am I being accused of something here?'

'No, not at all, Paul. We are just following lines of enquiry. I am going to show you another child. Can tell us if you recognise him?'

Rocco passed a photograph of Patrick Ward across the table.

'Yes. I think he is another one of the kids at the rink.'

Stacey had paid particular attention to how he answered that question. She noticed a sudden twitch in his right eye.

'How long have you worked at the ice rink, Paul?' asked Rocco.

'I've been there for seven years now. I love my job there and speaking to the parents and their children. Not to mention the hundreds of other people that come to the place. Groups, other clubs. Sometimes we have celebrities there, too.'

'Can you describe your relationship with Clara Thompson? How long you have known her and her family, please?' asked Stacey.

'Oh, I get it, now. Are you the bad cop?' He smiled. 'Yes. She was one of the kids who first started at the club. She is a very talented skater and everyone knows that about her.

So, I've known her about two and a half years, I guess. We get on really well. She has a great sense of humour, for one so young. She always makes fun of my beard.' replied Paul Horton.

'So what do you think happened, Paul? Why would such a young girl just disappear, do you think? Did you see anything odd, anything at all?' asked Rocco.

'No, nothing, I noticed her coming out of the changing room. She just waved as she left. She did seem to be in more of a hurry than usual, but I guess she was probably just hungry. You know what kids are like.'

Chapter

30

Maggie and Nate had been going through cold cases of missing children spanning eighteen years. They looked for any who fitted the descriptions of those recently reported as missing. Just to find a link. Anything. The slightest similarity. Or something close or interesting, no matter what, that might help.

As they went through the historic cases, both were interested to see that the age range of the children was between seven and ten years. More often than not, they had been reported missing from foster care homes and social care settings.

Nate created a new database to include names, dates of disappearance, identifying marks and living circumstances, as well the current outcome and status of each case, thus far. Working with Maggie, they had soon cross-referenced a set of details and similarities to each other, as well as the locations of disappearances of each child. It was uncanny. They soon noticed that the only significant difference was that, in the latest cases, the children had been taken over a shorter period.

Nate took their updated information to the next briefing. Rocco was impressed and asked him to present their findings to the team. He was also tasked to take a PC with him to visit every family or caregiver to get further details. They needed to add as much detail to the database as possible.

Nate had purposely left two columns at the end of the new database to be completed when he spoke to those connected with each missing child. He secured the file so that only the Galaxy team had access.

Under this ongoing line of enquiry, Maggie had been tasked with compiling a list of every social worker, support team and any children's services members of staff who had ever had any involvement with any child who had been reported missing within the last eighteen years. Contact and interviews would need to be conducted for each person on that list. This was a huge piece of work and would require extra staff to assist. A request had to be submitted up the chain of command. Maggie placed the request form on Rocco's desk. It was put on the top of the pile, clearly marked Urgent.

The first person to be contacted was Tracey Fletcher, a child support safeguarding officer. She was interviewed at length as her name had appeared more than once in Maggie's and Nates enquiries.

Tracey was a tall, thin, thirty-eight-year-old woman, who didn't take kindly to being questioned. After a detailed interview, she was thanked and released. Afterwards, having reviewed their notes, both Nate and Maggie were quick to notice that all of the Social Care Pre-Incident Risk Assessment forms had been signed off by the lead social care manager, Mrs Gloria Mountford. Rocco wanted to meet this lady. She would interview her personally.

At the same time that Tracey was being interviewed, intelligence had come through to the Galaxy team that made Rocco's heart skip a beat. It wasn't the first time that an elderly couple had been spotted enticing children into their car or to go with them.

The call had come from the forensic team who had been carefully looking through the CCTV footage from the sports centre. The team had requested that she look at a suspect who matched the description of the female who had abducted Harris Evans.

'Her name is Gloria Mountford, Ma'am. It's unlikely to be her, though. She's a social worker. She's supposed to be on our side, isn't she?' asked a junior member of the team.

'I want to be the first to question this woman. I'm sure I have come across her before on another case, years ago. From what I remember, she thinks she is above everyone else because of her status. I can't stand social workers at the best of times. Let's see who she really is, shall we? Mrs High and Bloody Mighty!'

Chapter

31

Harris and Leon had been put in a room together. They had been drugged, but by now, the effects had worn off. They stared at each other in total shock at their situation.

Albie was whispering from next door. 'Hey you two, are you okay? I'm going to try to get us out of here. Just talk to me, alright.'

There was no reply, just the sound of two children sobbing. Albie was a smart kid. His family were always stimulating him with new challenges and experiences. His dad had taken him on many adventures across the world. At eight years old, he had already experienced snorkelling, diving, metal detecting and, most recently, an 'Escape Room' adventure in the city.

Looking around the filthy room, where goodness knows how many other children had been, he couldn't see any obvious means of escape. But that didn't mean that he wasn't going to try and find one.

The red and gold flocked wallpaper was peeling from the walls because of the dampness. The smell caught in his throat. Earlier, he had figured out that, if he covered his nose and mouth with his t-shirt, it blocked some of the stench.

He could hear the boys in the next room coughing in between their sobs. They were suffering from more than being cooped up in this disgusting hole.

Albie ran his hand across the wall where the windows had been boarded up. There was enough light filtering through the tiny spaces in the wood for him to see that the boards had been screwed to the window frame.

He wondered what his dad would be saying now. He could hear him in his mind. He closed his eyes to see his face. He would be saying 'Think son, think. There must be a way out.'

Albie opened his eyes to let them adjust to the dim light. He felt for his belt. It was his grandfather's and was way too big for him. He remembered there was a thin metal band on it which his uncle Conrad had made to secure the slack so that he could wear it without looking completely weird. If he could just get that off he might be able to use it as a makeshift screwdriver to loosen the window boards.

A part of him was saying that it was pointless. He would never get free. But he was determined not to give in to that negativity. He banished that voice from his mind. He took his belt off and, somehow, managed to free the metal band from the leather belt. All he had to do now was break it apart. He remembered his grandad bending a piece of metal until it broke, much as he had seen his mum do with an old credit card. As he buckled the metal back and forth, he could feel the heat that it was generating. His frustration at being locked up gave him the determination to keep going. His fingers were hurting, but he didn't care. Abruptly he felt the metal give. It snapped apart.

Suddenly, he could hear keys rattling. He took a sharp breath. He slipped the two pieces of metal in his pocket and sat in the corner of the room.

There were loud voices outside the rooms. He could hear a boy screaming out 'I want my mummy! I want to go home!'

Albie put his head in his hands and cried. He had no idea where they were taking the boy or if he was going to be next or what was happening.

This whole experience was new to him. He had never, ever been forced to do anything in his young life. He'd always been asked as part of a discussion. He was frightened but he knew he had to hold onto hope, just a glimmer of hope that he would find a way to get himself and the other two boys out of here. Anger overtook fear at the injustice of what was happening in this house.

Despite his young age, he knew, he just knew, that this was bad. His mother was in the police. He was forbidden to read any of her files or listen in on her conversations. But when she was out or asleep, he couldn't help but sneak a peek.

Chapter

32

Holly sat in the stinking basement room, untethered but rigid with fear. And then. With a sudden jolt, she stood up. Although she had been keeping her muscles working every day as best she could, it still hurt to stand. Now, dressed in the warmer clothes, she could feel some life flowing back into her tiny body. She quietly dashed up the concrete stairs. It was now or never.

She reached for the door handle and the lock that she'd heard rattle so many times before. Each time she had been so appallingly violated.

She found the handle. The door was unlocked, as Annie had promised. She closed it gently behind her. She was out. Feeling her way down the long, dark hallway, she kept as close to the wall as she could get. A light went on further up the hallway. She froze on the spot.

Closing her eyes, and hardly daring to breathe, she waited. Nothing. Only the sound of her beating heart in her ears.

She carried on to the end of the hallway as Annie had instructed. She turned right. The side door was unlocked, just as her friend had said it would be.

She opened it. She was outside. The fresh air hit her like an icy blast. It was as if life itself was being pumped back into her. This gave her a renewed determination to succeed. There was no going back now. She found her way to the perimeter of the grounds and the high brick wall.

It was the middle of the night. Holly didn't look back. She focused on looking forward and soon found herself at the edge of a wood, where the end of the high wall ended. She just knew that she had to keep going.

Running through the woods, she couldn't see properly. She tripped and fell flat on her face. She lay still, silently pleading with the universe that no one or nothing had heard her. That she hadn't awakened a sleeping monster.

It was then that she remembered what the school counsellor had taught her. 'When you're having to deal with a difficult situation, pretend that you have a strong powerful animal with you.'

Holly started to imagine that there was a huge polar bear beside her. Together, they ran through the wood. After a while, she could see headlights in the distance and knew that she must be near a road.

Annie had told her to avoid being seen but to follow the road. By now, Holly was exhausted and had no idea where she was going. She made it across the road without being seen. Her eyes had started to adjust and she hurried into the next set of trees and overgrowth.

She hadn't travelled far before she had reached the top of a hill. From there she could just make out a small hut on the shoreline of a large lake. It was the sort of place where a shepherd might shelter from the rain. She had seen them while on a school trip to the Lake District.

If she could just get there she would be able to close her eyes and rest a bit. Maybe, then she could carry on for a few more hours before daybreak. She might only be seven years old but she knew that the revolting man at the house had a routine. Even though he hadn't been to hurt her for a day or so, he always did it in the morning, as soon as it was light. So she had to get as far away as she could in the dark before anyone noticed she was missing.

She had only one trainer now and her trousers were ripped from the sharp branches and trees. It felt like she had a thousand cuts and bruises.

On and on she went, not stopping until she reached the hut. It was empty, except for some straw and a strong smell of urine, not unlike where she had just been kept. Only this smelled like animal urine rather than her own or that of the many children who had been imprisoned in that room before her.

It would be safe for a while she thought. She sat down closest to the door, ready to run if she had to. She leaned back against the cold stone wall of the hut and closed her eyes.

The clothes she was wearing were stiff and uncomfortable. In the pocket of the jacket, she'd found a plastic zip bag. The light wasn't good but as her eyes adjusted she took it out and carefully opened it. In the bag, she found a twenty-pound note, a packet of fruit pastels, some chewing gum and six paracetamol capsules that had been carefully cut from a packet of twelve. She smiled for a second, then cried deep body sobs as she thought of Annie, still there in that dreadful place, being beaten and abused every single day.

Opening the fruit sweets she stuffed four into her mouth. She stopped herself from eating anymore because she had seen films where people stranded on a desert island had to ration what they had. She felt a twinge of guilt for having eaten four so quickly. As she put her stash back into her pocket she felt the fruit juice from the candy flow down the back of her throat, quenching her aching thirst just a tiny bit. Every part of her body felt as if it had been thrown against a wall. She ached inside and out. She knew that she had to keep strong, just for a while longer.

By now, Holly had been on the run for about six hours. She'd slept for an hour and then decided to keep going. She carried on up a hill away from the shepherds' hut. She was a tough kid, having cared for her mother from such an early age. But even so, her little body couldn't take much more. She was weak and tired.

All she could think about was that she had to get back home. To her mother and some sort of normality. As dawn broke, she felt exposed and more vulnerable than ever. She didn't look down as she ran, faster and faster. She tripped far and long over a raised rock, smashing her head on another. Holly lay unconscious in the cold and damp of the early morning dew.

Chapter

33

Police Interview

Mrs Gloria Mountford – Personal Account
Present: DCI Rochelle Raven, Sergeant Stacey
Lord, Mrs Gloria Mountford

Stacey accompanied Rocco to interview Mrs
Gloria Mountford. Right from the start, Rocco had
decided she didn't like the woman, her energy
didn't match her façade of her obnoxious self-
righteousness.

'Thank you, Mrs Mountford, for assisting us
with our enquiries today. We both have some
questions for you regarding six children who have
gone missing recently, in addition to several other
children who have disappeared over the last
eighteen years. We will try not to keep you for too
long.' said Rocco.

'So, Mrs Mountford, as far as you're aware,
were all of the Missing from Care Procedures
carried out correctly for the children for whom you

have signed the Missing Child Assessment records ?' asked Stacey.

'Yes, of course, they were. You know yourself, officer, from the social care procedures that we have followed it, to the letter. And, of course, we must always be aware and alert to the fact that some children are trafficked out of the UK very quickly. We do try to keep every child monitored but it isn't always easy. You can go through every form with a fine-tooth comb and I can assure you that you will not find anything untoward.' replied Gloria Mountford.

'Oh, we intend to, Mrs Mountford. We intend to do just that.' assured Rocco.

'Are you familiar with the name Holly Knowles, Mrs Mountford?' asked Stacey.

'Not without more information no. I can't. I'm sure that you can understand. I have hundreds of children on the registers. Can you give me further details?'

Rocco slid a photograph of the young Holly Knowles across to the woman. Picking it up, the woman peered at it from over her glasses. Her face was a mask, her self-control still in place.

'Well, that is not enough information. What is the child's background? Is she missing, as well? I mean, you can't expect me to just pull images from my mind. I've seen thousands of children over the years.'

'Yes, she is missing. She was caring for her mother who has multiple sclerosis. She was also in the social care system. Your team, I believe?' answered Stacey.

'Yes. Now, I do remember this one, actually. She was a disaster waiting to happen. No consistency. Continually caring for the mother. No nurturing or guidance. We visited on occasion and from what I can remember she was parent, teacher, carer, counsellor and child to herself and to her mother.

There can be no discipline when a child has all the responsibility. No doubt, she had access to the internet too. She probably just had enough of her mother and left the area. She was a pre-incident risk from the start of her involvement with us.' replied the woman.

'She is just a child, Mrs Mountford, just a child'. exclaimed Rocco, shocked by the woman's attitude.

'Look. If you don't mind, officers, I have a very busy schedule and I simply don't have time for these trivialities.' sneered Gloria Mountford.

'Can I remind you, Mrs Mountford that six children of similar ages have gone missing within eight weeks? Your name is present on every document that is connected with each child. I have a few more questions before we can conclude this meeting. Let's go through the pre-incident risk assessment and pre-review reports again shall we.' said Rocco, with authority.

'I don't like what you're implying, officer, but, for now, I will assist where I can.' replied Gloria Mountford, looking down her nose at the officers.

'Okay. So can you tell us how the system works, in simple terms, please?' asked Stacey.

'The pre-incident risk assessment, where it is necessary, needs to be reviewed regularly as part of the social worker's pre-review report. In those cases where there are serious concerns about the risk of a child or young person going missing, we always need to consider informing the police and other relevant local authority. You know that we have always shared information with you and all other agencies.' replied the woman.

'Mrs Mountford, none of the involved children under the safeguarding protocols of the social care system have ever been reported missing. We're not talking about teenagers here. We're talking about seven to nine-year-olds. These are urgent enquiries and we will not stop until each and every child has been found. Dead or alive.'

'I can assure you that all social workers under my management are supervised and are regularly appraised. Any insubordination would be flagged up to me and severely dealt with.'

When they had gone as far as they could, the police officers stopped their informal questioning and allowed Mrs Mountford to leave. She was told that, should a formal interview be required, she would most likely require a solicitor.

'Stacey, don't you think that was a strange thing to say. Insubordination. I mean, who fucking says that, in this day and age!' said Rocco, shaking her head.

Stacey looked at her boss in silence, her expression mirroring her boss's incredulity as they cleared their desk to leave the interview room.

Back at her office, Rocco spoke to her head administrator. 'Mags, this shockingly shit! How can these children keep going missing right under our noses? What are we missing here?'

Mags listened, empathising with her boss's frustration. She was taking notes and trying to be helpful, placating where necessary. They were all exhausted and frustrated at their lack of progress.

Chapter

34

The crew aboard the police search helicopter was on the lookout for a young man called Jason Warrington, who had just escaped from Hellasay North High-Security Prison.

The man focused the searchlight on what he had first thought was a dead calf on the grassy banks, not more than a mile from the lake. As he zoomed in with the camera, the operator noticed small feet and shouted to the pilot 'Get me down there, now! It's a kid! It's a kid.'

The helicopter immediately turned and began a rapid descent. Finding a clearing, they were able to land. The pilot cut the engine.

When they reached the child, they could see that she'd been in trouble. Her skin was barely visible through the blood, dirt, black bruises and cuts all over her little body. Her eyes were rolling and she was trying to say something that sounded like 'dolly, dolly'. The child was about the same age as his own daughter and his paternal instincts kicked into overdrive.

He lifted Holly in his arms and carried her over to the helicopter. Gently placing her on the stretcher, he strapped her in. He raised his arm, swirling his wrist to the pilot, signalling for him to lift off. Within seconds, they were on their way to the hospital.

The pilot called the job into the operator back at headquarters to ensure that they would be able to have immediate access to the helipad at the hospital. The operator confirmed availability and that there was a medical team who would be on standby to meet them.

'It's okay, little one. We'll soon have you safe and sound. We'll find out who you are and get hold of your parents.' he said gently, stroking the child's face with his gloved hand.

Chapter

35

Gloria remembered an article or a blog that she had read earlier in the year. It discussed how children were primarily targeted by those who had access to them, authorised or otherwise.

It revealed that sexual predators who preyed upon children frequently secured positions of authority or trust or were already family members, friends or relations. In the guise of everyday interaction, sexual predators groom, coerce, manipulate, dominate, ridicule, threaten or isolate their victims, and indeed their families, in subtle but targeted approaches. These behaviours can occur over days, months or even years, gradually wearing away any resistance or empowerment. Nothing was altruistic or accidental in the world of the sexual predator.

It made her smile and cynically wonder if the author was actually a part of the 'group' or if they genuinely did care about the welfare of these children. She had seen it all before in her many years as a social worker.

In her warped view, people who genuinely cared were few and far between.

The Access Auction, as she had called it, was due to take place in a few weeks. She had almost reached her quota of children. They were stored and ready. She was going to make sure that, as soon as the auction was over, she would be gone, leaving that pathetic husband of hers to rot in that rat-infested house. She knew she was running out of time. She had a plan and it was to be far far away from him.

When Gloria Mountford returned to Magpie House, after the informal meeting with those ghastly policewomen, she was in a foul mood. She had just about had enough of people poking around in her business.

'Annie, get up here. Now! We have to move some of those little brats about. Where is that useless man?' demanded Gloria.

Lance Mountford appeared at the door and ushered Annie in front of him.

'Get me a gin. Now!' shouted Gloria to the child.

'Whatever is wrong, my dear?' asked the old man.

'Those bloody police! That's what's wrong! They were all over me today, like a rash.

We're going to have to move some of these children on. Clear them out, or something. Just until it's all over. I mean, just how many are we storing in that cellar these days? Have you even been down there to look?'

'Okay. I can see why you're angry, my dear. Now, have that drink and let's work out what we're going to do. The Access Auction is in a few weeks from now. Surely we can hold them off until then?' offered Lance, trying to place his wife.

'Oh, I don't know. They seemed pretty sure that I am involved somehow.'

Gloria had started to calm down, compliments of the gin and Lance's calming tone. She gestured for Annie to sit and wait for her orders.

'Right. We will start by contacting those who have already purchased a child. Any that we are keeping here, especially for your horrible little man in the woods, will have to go. Let them take responsibility for the creatures. I will be charging them for storage, anyway. I don't want the hassle or the risk any longer.'

Chapter

36

His wife had passed out from all the gin she had consumed. Now, he was going to take his rage out on his latest child victim. But, within minutes, he was storming back up the steps. Lance Mountford was raging.

'How the fuck can she have got out? It's that little bastard's doing, I bet. Where is she? Where's Annie?' screamed Lance Mountford as he paced up and down the drawing-room in a blind fury. His booming voice echoed throughout the house.

'I knew we should have drowned that ugly little bitch at birth. She was never going to bring us any money, with a face like that. To think we gave her a purpose, a job! Wait till I get my hands on her this time.' screamed Lance, spit flying in all directions.

He checked the room again, searching all the adjoining spaces. She was nowhere to be found. That door needed fixing. He had been trapped down there a few times now. It was on his to-do list.

He suddenly remembered that there was quite a lot to do in that cellar. He must get on to it. After the auction. Yes, he would do it then. Focusing on his mental to-do list seemed to calm him down. He went back up to the drawing-room and poured himself a generous glass of whiskey.

Chapter

37

Once, while rooting around in the basement where Holly Knowles had been kept, Annie had discovered a separate partition. Through a concealed, inner door there was a dark black cubby hole. It was perfect for her plans.

She had snatched time over the previous few months, to clean it out. She had found a white translucent nightdress in one of the bags of clothes that her mother frequently brought home. She was in no doubt that their contents had been intended for charity shops, but had been appropriated by her mother.

Annie wanted to look the part when her time came and she wanted to get it right. To get something right once in her short life. Her faith in God was her strength. She genuinely believed that he would save her. She wanted to be ready for the moment when He did. Annie had been hoarding some of the medication meant for the other children over months of careful planning. She was resigned to her chosen fate.

She downed the cocktail of red lemonade and vodka, which contained the tramadol and paracetamol tablets that she'd crushed into a fine powder earlier that morning.

As she lay on the cold concrete, she felt a warmth and peace flood her entire body. She closed her eyes.

'I hope Holly makes it. I hope she saves them all' she prayed to herself, as tears rolled down her cheeks and onto her hare lip.

This world was no longer a place she wanted to be. She couldn't handle any more pain or abuse. But, more importantly, she just couldn't be party to any more abuse of innocent children by those monsters upstairs. She wanted to be with God. She wanted to go home to Him.

Her beliefs and conviction gave her comfort. As she drifted off, she heard the most beautiful sound, like a harp. Soft voices, angelic and joyful, filled the air. Light shone through her and all around the room, through the tiny gaps in the window boards and into her heart as she floated into a soft and safe world, where she watched herself taking a high dive off of the top of a vast canyon.

Chapter

38

Three nurses and a doctor were on standby, awaiting the helicopter's arrival. As they landed on the dedicated helipad, the young girl was speedily carried through the hospital doors and into a separate room in the ICU department.

The girl was hanging on by a thread, she was alive but she was unresponsive. Examination revealed that she was hypoglycaemic, with dangerously low blood pressure. She was severely dehydrated and hypothermic. The medical team covered her with heated blankets and began intravenous drips to counteract the dehydration and hypotension, as well as the hypoglycaemia.

While the nurses and doctors continued their treatments, the police and the local safeguarding team were notified of the unidentified child who had been brought in to the emergency unit in a life-threatening condition.

Within seventy-two hours, Holly had regained consciousness. A police officer was waiting at her bedside. 'Hello, my name is Stacey. What's your name?'

'Holly. I am Holly and I want my mummy. Is she alive? Where is she?' whispered the child, who was becoming increasingly agitated.

'Everything is okay. I can find your mummy, but first, you need to tell me your full name. That will make it easier for me to find her, okay?'

'Knowles. My name is Holly Knowles.' cried the child as she drifted back into a deep sleep.

'I'm sorry officer, but we must let the child sleep. She is physically and psychologically exhausted. She can barely string two sentences together right now. We have had to medicate her to give her the best chance of recovery.' interrupted the Paediatric Nurse Specialist.

'Okay. But I need to get a full report from whoever bought her in. And we will need a police guard at the hospital room door, at all times'

'Yes of course. Who is this poor child?'

'You will know soon enough.' replied Stacey, as she left the room and headed out to the car park.

When the nurse returned, she noticed that Holly's cheeks had become mottled. Her lips had turned a bluish colour. She was breathing in short sharp rasps. The nurse immediately lifted the girl's gown to discover that a rash was spreading over her body. Pressing the emergency buzzer, the other nurses came rushing in.

The wounds on Holly's feet and legs had become infected. She had developed sepsis. It had developed from the contaminated conditions in the shepherd's hut that she had slept in, as well as from the soil she had run through. It was now touch and go for this little girl.

Chapter

39

The European magpie is notorious for stealing shiny objects. Magpies are attracted to ladies' jewellery, plastics and even the windscreen wipers from cars. The magpie will often take the objects it has found and hoard them in its nest. Magpies are highly intelligent birds and are often able to sense approaching danger very quickly. They are also known to be sociable and curious birds but become reclusive when they sense danger. They are known for their long memories, especially for anyone who has harmed them in the past.

Lance and Gloria Mountford lived in the huge mansion, which had been purchased with their ill-gotten gains from years of child procurement and trafficking. Lance had never really worked, per se. He'd had occasional work, mostly under the table jobs, which co-existed with his wheeling and dealing. Any legitimate work, such as his office in the centre of town, was a façade for his illegal businesses. He was adept at maintaining a low profile, content to let his wife take any limelight that her job offered.

They had both been born in the small market town of Great Shawley and had attended the same school; childhood sweethearts. They had grown and indulged their collective depravity, sharing many of the same interests and compulsions. They were homebodies, rarely moving from their birthplace, just like the magpie. And like magpie pairs, they were completely and utterly devoted to each other. Or so he thought.

Gloria was an experienced social worker who, over the last ten years, had worked her way up to a high profile job as Chief Executive Officer of a specialist charity for children who had been left without parents after murder or manslaughter. The charity was called 'By Their Side' and it provided online and face to face advice and support for its clients. There was play therapy for pre-schoolers and weekly drop-in sessions and organised outings for any older children. Funding was primarily secured from government sources. However, other income streams included the national lottery and private and corporate donations. The charity was also a regular recipient of not-insignificant anonymous donations.

Gloria was well respected in her field, so much so, that many organisations, government offices and police departments sought her knowledge and expertise, especially when updating their safeguarding policies and developing new training programmes.

She had single-handedly created a safeguarding programme called The Children's Chapter, which was a new and innovative approach to opening up a pathway for children to be adopted abroad. On paper, it had been designed with safety as a key element, but without the red tape that often made the traditional adoption process so long and cumbersome, a process which was sometimes responsible for further psychological damage to both the children and potential adoptive parents alike. It included intercounty and domestic approaches while being open to prospective adopters from the local authority.

It was to be overseen by social services safeguarding department, headed by Mrs Gloria Mountford. Working with agencies involved in or signed up to The Children's Chapter allowed her oversight of all steps in the process with international partner agencies. Part of its remit was to advise local authorities in cases where children were being placed abroad.

She was well-regarded by her peers. She was, in every way, a highly respected woman.

Two years earlier, she had received a Dame Hood for her significant, long term contribution as a senior social work chief. She didn't give it much credence. The award sat on the mantel in the drawing-room, a testament to her ability to control and deceive.

Chapter

40

Knocking on the front door of Holly Knowles' house, Rocco was welcomed by Heather Knowles and also Clara's parents and grandmother. Sophie Dalton was asleep on the sofa. Jenny, the liaison officer, was making hot drinks for everyone.

'Hello, Inspector Raven. Is there any news? It's not like you to visit us unannounced.' said Clara's mother, desperately expectant.

'Yes, we have some good news. We have found Holly and she is alive, but she is in a bad way at the moment. I have come to take you to her.'

Mrs Knowles fell to the floor in relief, her weakened body unable to sustain her. Rocco helped her to the table and encouraged her to have a drink. After she had taken in the news, Rocco instructed Jenny to help Mrs Knowles get ready to go to the hospital. Rocco and Stacey would accompany her.

'But no news of our Clara then, officer?' asked Mrs Thompson.

'Not yet, I'm afraid. But once we speak to Holly we will know more, no doubt.' Rocco reassured the desperate mother.

Rocco, Stacey and Mrs Knowles left the house and into the waiting car. When they arrived at the hospital Stacey prepared Heather Knowles for what they might find. Jenny was told to return to the other parents and to continue as normal.

The general ward was noisy with catering trolleys, and the usual dings and dongs of a busy ward. There was a strong smell of disinfectant. Stacey guided Heather Knowles' wheelchair through the melee.

The ICU was a complete contrast to the ward that they had just navigated. The only noises were the beeping of machines and the swooshing of ventilators. After being buzzed in by the receptionist, Stacey asked for Holly Knowles. They were ushered to take a seat and informed that a doctor would be with them as soon as possible.

Stacey's heart ached for Heather. She prayed that the child hadn't died. She had looked quite grey when Stacey had left her earlier. Thinking about it, nothing would have surprised her.

A tall fair-haired man in a white gown appeared and came over to Heather and Stacey.

'Ah hello. My name is Doctor Matthew Jacobs. And you must be Holly's mother?'

'Yes, that's right. I'm her mum. This is Sergeant Stacey Lord. She has kindly brought me here to see my daughter. Where is she? Is she okay?'

'Yes, yes, she is okay at the moment. But I'm afraid she really has been through the wars and has contracted sepsis as a result. This is a very dangerous condition, as I'm sure you are aware. She has some very strong antibiotics running through her system at the moment. Hopefully, they will fight off the infection. And all we can do is wait and hope that she pulls through. She is monitored constantly and is currently showing all positive signs.' replied the doctor.

'Can I see her?' asked Heather.

'We really don't want to aggravate her condition or for her to get distressed. I know this is difficult, but could I respectfully ask that you come back when she wakes up. I will call you personally.'

Heather Knowles didn't seem to know what to say. She was so happy that her daughter was alive. She would do whatever it took to help her.

'I'm sorry to have to ask this of you, I really am. Please let us look after Holly and we will be in touch as soon as she wakes up.'

When Stacey asked if the police could help, the doctor turned to her. 'Actually, there is something I need to tell you. Stacey, did you say your name was? Just give me a moment, please.'

The doctor disappeared into the ICU ward. Stacey noticed that Heather was crying.

'What if she doesn't wake up, Stacey? I just wanted to see my baby, just once.'

The doctor reappeared and asked Stacey if she knew anyone with the name Raven in the police force.

'Yes, she is our Commanding Officer, Doctor Jacobs. Why do you ask?'

'One of our nurses found this in Holly's jeans pocket. Thought it might be important.' he replied.

'Look, I know what you've said is crucially important but is there any way that Heather could just see her daughter, even for a moment? We can keep our distance. I will just wheel her in. She just wants to see her, that's all. She has been missing for so long.'

The doctor looked from Stacey to Heather and back again. 'Okay, come with me. Now, you won't be able to stay for very long, just a few minutes. Please don't say anything or let her have any sense that you are upset.' replied the doctor.

The wheelchair glided silently along the spotless blue speckled flooring of the ICU ward where Holly Knowles was attached to an oxygen mask and several IV infusions.

Heather smiled at the doctor and mouthed a 'Thank you.' She nodded to Stacey, and they left just as quietly as they had entered.

'I just needed to see her. To know she is alive and that is hope enough for me, Stacey. Hope is everything.'

Chapter

41

It was ten o'clock in the morning. The office was buzzing and stress levels were through the roof.

'Roc, it's Mike, I've got Alan Markham here, the vet from the high street. He's here at the house with George, his son. You know Albie's mate from school. I think you'd better get over here now.'

'I'm on my way.' replied Rocco, with an equalled sense of urgency.

Without speaking to anyone, Rocco left the station and raced to Mike's house. As she walked in, the tension was palpable. She scanned the room. Alan and his son were seated at the kitchen table with Mike. Alan looked angry and she could see that George had been crying. The little boy's head was bowed, his eyes glued to an invisible speck on floor.

'Hey George, what's going on? Why have you been crying?' asked Rocco as she gently laid her hand on his shoulder.

'He's got something to tell you. Haven't you, son?' Alan was staring at his son.

'I'm so sorry. I'm sorry, I'm sorry. It was all my idea!' wailed the young boy, as tears and snot ran down his face.

'Get on with it.' demanded Alan.

Rocco butted in, trying to diffuse the tension. 'It's okay, George. Come on, now. Take your time and just tell me what's happened. Do you know where Albie is?'

Mike let his ex-wife do all the talking. She had a way with children, as well as getting to the truth.

George was stuttering in between his sobs. 'Albie and I broke into my dad's clinic. We took his keys when he was away on business and mum was out shopping for the day with Auntie Rene. We injected one of his new pet tracking microchips into each other's arms. It was just meant to be a laugh to see if we could find each other on our phones. We didn't mean to hurt anyone, I swear. I'm really, really sorry.'

Rocco suddenly smiled and looked across at Mike, his face the picture of confusion. Then suddenly, his eyes widened. Their visitors were arguing at the table, the father chastising the boy for his dangerous and irresponsible behaviour.

'Hang on a minute, Alan. This could be the best news ever.

Tell me more about these microchips. What are they used for? How do they work?' Rocco's excitement was building.

'Well, they are a relatively new global positioning system set up by the RSPCA and Dog Breeders Association UK and Ireland. As the demand for more exotic puppies and kittens grows, so do their price. They become more and more valuable to thieves. These GPS microchips enable us to track the dog's location by satellite, in the event of theft or even if they run off.' replied Alan, now realising why Rocco was so interested.

Mike took a deep breath. 'Okay, okay. So if Albie has one of these trackers under his skin there's a chance that we'll be able to trace him, won't we? And find out exactly where he is. Is this what you're telling us?'

'Yes, it is. But only if we have the serial numbers.' replied Alan, looking at his son.

'What do you mean? asked Rocco.

'Well, Rocco, essentially, this is how it works. For every animal we add to the GPS database we have to complete and submit full documentation about the animal, the breeder and the owner's details.' replied Alan.

George sat in silence, still with his head down, still focused on that invisible speck. His legs swung nervously underneath the table. Mike got up from the table and returned with tissues, a chocolate bar and a glass of milk. Mike's instinctive ability to soothe the child did not go unnoticed. Rocco smiled. More than ever, she knew what a great dad he was. She saw the dark circles and redness around his eyes, swollen from lack of sleep and fear and despair.

Apart from odd visits to the Mill, Mike hadn't left the house in case Albie might return on his own. He had left the searching to the Galaxy team and the additional officers and volunteers. It was clear to Rocco that every second their son was missing, he, like her, was being torn apart.

'Okay, Alan. Now, we all must think clearly. I need to see this system and how it works. George, did you record the serial numbers?' asked Rocco, her focus switching from Alan to the boy.

'We threw the packaging in the big green garden bin, Mrs Raven. I am so sorry.' sobbed George.

Rocco called the office and asked Maggie to instruct Nate Bridges to drop everything immediately and to get his body camera equipment and meet her at Moorland Vets as soon as possible. She asked her to send Hesh and Stacey to the Markham house and to make sure that they were also wearing their bodycams. She wanted them to search through the large green waste disposal bins for any trace of the packaging belonging to the GPS trackers. They had to have those serial numbers.

Mike had agreed to stay at the house while Rocco met her team at the veterinary practice. Alan was to drop George off at home, then meet them there.

Nate was already at the practice when they arrived. They went directly to Alan's office at the rear of the building. Alan had also realised that the boys' prank could inadvertently turn out to be the best lead in the case. He carefully entered the password for the programme. He explained to Nate how the system worked. Nate made himself comfortable and took over the keyboard. Everything he did was being seen by the Galaxy team at Head Office via his body camera, where Mark and Maggie were watching and recording. He began by trawling through the serial numbers for any that hadn't been allocated.

'So what you're saying then, Mr Markham, is that all the numbers are on the database and the Global Positioning System tracking device is in place. It's just that, without the correct serial number, it's impossible to match the microchip to the corresponding animal, or in this case, child?' enquired Nate.

'Yes, that's exactly how it works.' The vet replied.

As this was a relatively new system, there were only thirteen unallocated serial numbers listed, four of which were where vets had failed to inject the microchip properly, meaning that they were invalid. The affected microchips had been returned to their packet and resealed. That left nine unallocated. Nate and Rocco sat tirelessly going through the nine serial numbers. They interrogated the reception staff while waiting for a call from Hesh and Stacey.

Four hours later, Hesh called in to report that he had sent an image on WhatsApp of what they'd found, in case they couldn't see them clearly from the body cam images. There were two packets with foil lining which appeared to be untouched. The paper covers were still intact but not completely legible due to water damage. Rocco read out what she thought was 25*89430*004 and 25*8943**6005.

She handed the phone to Nate to see if he could figure it out. He tried numerous combinations by using the missing numbers from one sequence and adding new numbers.

Rocco moved away from the desk as Mike was calling on her mobile. He was desperate to know if anything had changed, if there was any news. Conrad, Martin and Niamh were still at her house, all waiting for news. They were taking turns to sleep and eat.

Niamh was sat in Albie's room admiring the artwork which he had made from plastic collected on the beach. It was an image of whales jumping out of the sea. She was in awe of the obvious talent and creativity of her beautiful nephew. Her heart was breaking. She was willing him to come home.

Conrad was in the kitchen, helping Martin to cook an Irish stew for dinner and generally keeping an eye on everyone.

Rocco could hear the warmth and love in Mike's voice as he spoke to her on the phone. She was so grateful for the family that she had waiting at home, praying for her to find their boy. It was at times like this when the family was together that she most missed the comforting presence of her mum and dad. Yet she knew that, wherever they were, they would be willing her to find him too.

She had already been warned off the case by Trenchie, who was worried about her. But Rocco knew that she had to find Albie herself. She had to be there to wrap him in her arms and never let him go. And find him she would, even if it was the last thing she ever did.

In the privacy of the office toilet, Rocco broke down in tears as the stress and tension overwhelmed her. She allowed herself to sit for a few moments, and then she stood up and splashed her face in cold water and dried her eyes. She reapplied her makeup, took several deep breaths, straightened her back and calmly walked towards the office, as if nothing had just happened.

Rocco heard a loud beep, similar to that of a submarine sonar system. She raced into Alan's office. She saw Nate punch the air, as he shouted 'Yes!'. The sound had been in response to the last combination that he'd entered into the computer.

It matched one of the serial numbers that had been unallocated. He switched the tracking device into monitoring mode and they waited. Within seconds, four strong beeps indicated that they had tracked the microchip. Nate typed in the coordinates. Alan came into the office as the printer spat out the document.

'You've tracked him, yes!' Alan exclaimed.

'What is your home address, Mr Markham?' asked Nate.

'52 Longley Avenue, BN16 0PZ' he replied.

'Looks like this is the microchip in your son's arm. He needs to be brought here so we can verify the number. Do you have a microchip reader here?' challenged Nate.

'Yes. Let me get it for you.'

'Well then, the next number has to be Albie's.' shouted Rocco, barely able to contain her excitement. She started pacing the room, her hands continuously running through her long black hair.

'Yes, it should be. Give me a minute.' said Nate. They all waited, staring at the screen.

Alan returned with the reader, which looked like a credit card machine. His wife had arrived with George. Alan sat his son on the chair as Nate scanned his arm with the reader.

'How big is the chip?' asked Nate, curiously.

'They used to be about the size of a grain of rice before the GPS device was added. But now they are about the size of a Rice Crispie. The more I think about it, the more I'm amazed how they managed to do it, to be honest.'

Beeeep! Beeeeep! Beeeeep! Beeeeep! confirmed the location of the next chip in the sequence.

'That's Longfield Lane. It's that fucking Magpie House! I knew that bastard bitch was lying!' screamed Rocco, as she grabbed her coat and headed for the door. She ordered Nate to activate the Search and Rescue Rapid Response Team immediately.

She wasted no time in contacting Trenchie to get authorisation for more backup. She knew they would find children in that house. It was a gut feeling, but she knew she was right.

Chapter

42

The Access Auction had been a roaring success as far as Gloria and Lance Mountford were concerned. The group of children who had been recently acquired had commanded some of the highest prices they had ever acquired. Some of the children they had kept in the cellar had been brought upstairs as a backup but they, too, had all sold in the frenzied bidding. Annie had certainly earned her keep on this day. It was she who had kept all the children fed, healthy and clean, at least well enough to be attractive to the buyers. Gloria had decided to give Annie a little reward but hadn't been able to find her.

The bidding had been incredibly close. Gloria had nearly sold Leon Dalton to an Iranian couple. Lance stopped her in the nick of time, as that boy had been promised to a certain Richard Murphy, who, by chance, had arrived at Magpie House a day earlier. Lance had given him one of the spare rooms. While Lance wined and dined with the rest of the guests, Richard had kept himself to himself.

As they prepared to leave with their purchases, each of those who had attended was chortling and laughing on the gravel drive as they got to their cars.

Paul Horton, in his new red sports car, was about to leave his wife, even though she had no idea. He was packed and ready to head off with his precious booty. He was startled by the screech of sirens and the flashing of the distinctive blue lights.

Rocco, Stacey and the rest of the team had travelled in separate cars. She had given orders for all body-worn cameras to be on at all times. Maggie and a couple of extra cops had been drafted in to keep watch over the whole incident from the unit headquarters. Trenchie was watching from a seat just behind Maggie and together they recorded every single minute of footage.

The laughter and sociability changed into a deathly silence. Panic set in. Like rats jumping from a sinking ship, they tried to escape. Police cars descended onto the drive, their tyres skidding on the gravel and flicking up stones as the mayhem commenced. Cars screeched to a halt, and officers jumped out to make their arrests.

The first person Rocco and the team saw was Paul Horton, with a little blonde girl of about ten years old. Two officers raced over. He seemed to be in shock. As the officers cuffed him, he collapsed onto the ground, wailing like a baby.

The child was quickly but gently taken into a waiting police car.

Rocco spotted Gloria Mountford with a red-haired man with a full red beard. His leather jacket, with matching trousers and hard, heavy motorcycle boots looked more like a fancy dress costume, rather than the uniform of a member of the notorious Hell's Angels. He was stopped in his tracks. He had been about to shove a young frightened Albie into the boot of his top of the line Range Rover.

Chaos ensued as people ran from their cars, leaving children standing alone and crying. Dogs barked and engines roared as people tried to escape through the bank of police cars that lined the drive.

As the carnage continued, officers were shouting 'Get down! Get down! Stop!' Hesh Cole arrested Richard Murphy in the nick of time as he was about to get into the back of a van with Leon Dalton. Hesh called out to a young female PC called Veronica to take the frightened child to her police car and not to let him out of her sight.

Two ambulances were on standby at the huge iron gates, blocking any exit, which only heightened the panicked buyers. Some of them had ran out from the back of the property but police officers with dogs were already lining the high wall. All escape routes had been completely covered.

Rocco wasn't going to take any chances in letting anyone get away. Her team had worked too hard and for far too long on this case.

Stacey Lord arrested Gloria Mountford. She was pleading insanity even before she'd been put into a car. She was shouting the same defence all the while she was being processed at the station. Her pleas had fallen on deaf ears.

The team had arrested four women and eight men, in total. But Lance Mountford was nowhere to be found.

People seemed to be milling about everywhere as the initial search team landed at Magpie House. Thirty-six police officers with four detection and cadaver dogs were ordered to search the property. The blue wash of the emergency and vehicles reflected on the ground in the teeming rain, as they swirled in their plastic casings.

As Rocco spotted her son, she called out to him. He ran straight into her arms, crying and so, so relieved to be free.

'Mum, Mum, Mum, I thought I'd never see you again.' he cried, sobbing into his mother's shoulder.

'Come on sweets. Let's get in the car. We'll ring your dad. He will be so happy to know that you are safe.' she whispered to him.

'There are so many more in there, Mum. You have to save them. I can show you where they are if you want?'

'No way. You're not going back in that house nor out of mine or your dad's sight, ever again. Did anyone hurt you? Touch you in any way? You know what I mean.'

'I'm okay Mum. Five minutes later though, and I would have been taken away with that man with the red beard. He bought me at the child auction. I was terrified, Mum. I'm so sad for the others though, because I don't know if they got away already or if they've been taken.'

Rocco felt sick to her stomach but she couldn't let her son see her distress.

'An auction! We had a lead about an auction earlier on in the case. Okay, Albie my darling. Hard as it is, one of the team will have to take a statement from you. I'm not allowed to do it.' Albie nodded.

'We *are* going to save them Albie, every last one of them, I promise you. For now, though, you must go home with your dad. Everyone else is waiting at the Mill. Just until I've finished this, okay? Then we will be together, all of us?'

Albie gave his mum an awkward smile. He had some understanding of what her job entailed.

Watching the arrests and commotion unfold from the car window, Rocco called Mike. 'Here's your dad, now Albie.' said Rocco, as the call she'd been waiting for came in.

'Yes Mike, he's here with me now, in my car. Look I'm sorry but you're going to have to come and get him. I can't leave the crime scene right now. There are loads of other children in there.' said Rocco, impatient to get back to the team.

'You're truly unbelievable! Do you know that? That job will be the death of you. It really will.' Mike shouted into the phone. His frustration boiling over, he waited to be passed to their son.

Rocco left them talking for a minute as she stepped out of the car to get a quick update from Stacey. She was torn between her job and never wanting to leave Albie ever again. She got back in the car and she and her son waited together until Mike arrived.

'Can you go over to the Mill, please? Con, Martin and Niamh are there waiting for us. I'll see you there later?' she asked Mike.

Her ex-husband, not wanting to fight, nodded to her as he hugged their son. He was filled with immense relief at having his son back. She waved as they drove off together. And once they were out of sight, Rocco was finally able to let out a scream, relieving the pent up pressure within her.

Two officers immediately ran towards her. She held out her hand to gesture them to stop. 'I'm okay, I'm okay. I just thought he was dead. But he's alive and safe. Now I need to get in there and find out where the rest of the bastards are that did this heinous thing to my son and the other children like him.' said Rocco, breathlessly. She took a couple of breaths deep into her lungs, stood up straight, then walked purposely towards the house.

Two officers escorted her inside so that she could investigate what had been happening and report back via the camera. She put in another request for back up from the Scene of Crime Unit and the canine unit. She was in no doubt that her request would be given immediate approval. This was an unprecedented situation on an unparalleled scale.

Chapter

43

Hesh was searching the east wing of the house. He knew he shouldn't have gone in without backup, but his instinct was leading him like a bloodhound. He found a door with a solid steel handle, similar to those found on walk-in industrial refrigerators. He pulled with all his strength. Finally, the hinges screeched, further evidence of the poor maintenance which characterised this tired dilapidated house, in which so many secrets lay. As he entered the room, the door behind him clicked shut, leaving him in complete darkness. He went back up the stairs and tried to find the door handle. There wasn't one. He was trapped.

He knew that he should never have ventured down there alone. He heard his father's and his grandfather's voices in his head, telling him what a fool he'd been.

Walking precariously down the stairs, he realised that he was in a cold sweat. He put one hand against the damp wall to steady himself. The invisible foggy mustiness, sickness and ammonia filled the air. He had to keep telling himself that he would be okay. Just breathe. Keep calm. Slowly to the bottom of the stairs, one step at a time. He had to find where that smell was coming from. Be brave. Be brave.

Finally, he reached the floor. Complete silence, then a sound like the mewling of a kitten. He walked towards the direction of the sound, suddenly remembering that he had a small clicker torch on the keyring that his wife had bought him for Christmas.

He recalled the time he had opened the gift to find the keyring. He remembered laughing and teasing his wife that she had found it in a Christmas cracker. He remembered chortling as if she hadn't bought him anything of worth, joking around with her. He felt in his pocket. He grasped the little cylindrical object in his fingers. He pulled it out and clicked the 'On' button. The sight before him made him reel backwards.

Children of all ages were chained in concrete stalls. Small brick walls about four feet high, separated them so that they could hear, but not see each other. He noted their eyes, sunken and ringed with darkness. Some of the children hid their eyes from the tiny bright light.

As he shone the small torch along the walls in the cellar, he noticed that some of the children were in pairs. Some were fully clothed, some half-dressed while others were completely naked. All of the children were filthy and either crying softly or staring into space. Others appeared to be asleep. Bowls of water were scattered across the floor and Hesh wasn't sure if these were meant for drinking or if they were the source of the ammonia smell.

The cellar seemed to go on and on. He whispered to the children that help was on the way.

As he continued making his way through this horror scene, a young girl, no more than ten years old, pointed to the right. She immediately averted her eyes as if expecting to be told off. He nodded to her and followed her direction, whispering that he would return in a minute or two.

The small dim ray of light from the torch revealed more and more stone boxes, which looked like dog cages. These were attached to the walls. Children filled every space. He had to use his shirt sleeve to mask the smell and to stop himself from gagging. He tried his radio again but there was nothing. He turned the volume up to the highest level. He kept it like that, in case it decided to burst into action.

There were more doors ahead. But he couldn't risk leaving the children he had already found, in case he couldn't get back to them. He needed to get help for them first. The children, who by now had begun to realise that this man wasn't another abuser, began to cry for help.

As their cries became louder, Hesh tried to calm them down. Suddenly he heard the sound of the big door creaking. He quickly retraced his steps, making his way back to the wooden stairway. He kept himself hidden, hoping he was not about to be discovered.

He switched off the tiny light. By now, the door had fully opened and he saw the welcome face of Sergeant Stacey Lord. His heart skipped a beat, such was his relief. She shone a torch down the stairs and, as the beam of light caught his face, she shouted down to him.

'Hesh! Jeez, is that you?'

'Stacey, whatever you do, don't let the door shut. It has no handle on the inside. Prop it open and get a team down here as quick as you can. There are children everywhere.'

'Leave it with me. I'll be straight back. Jesus Christ, what is that smell?'

'Just hurry up, Stace. You'll soon see for yourself. You're not going to believe this.'

It felt like an eternity to Hesh, but within twenty minutes Stacey Lord returned with a standby team of ten fully kitted out, search-and-rescue crew and their equipment. They carried portable lighting and foil blankets and were being followed in by a further team of paramedics carrying stretchers and even more blankets.

Stacey looked around at the atrocity before her. She had never seen anything like it.

Using a small generator, the team worked quickly to set the lights up in as many cleared places as they could find. With military precision, fire crew and police officers cut the chains off the terrified children and freed them from their bonds. Paramedics took over the care of each child, wrapping each in a blanket with foil lining, then passing them up the stairway along the human chain into waiting ambulances.

Doctors and nurses were on standby at the Harbury Queens Medical Centre for the unprecedented emergency that had been called in over an hour ago. The first eighteen children were brought in as if in slow motion. They were clearly in deep shock, eyes wide open but vacant. They were followed by the others, some walking, others wrapped in foil blankets and being carried by fire crew, paramedics or police.

The team had discovered twenty-eight children in the stinking prison cellar. There had been older children between nine and ten years of age who had been tied to walls in separate stalls, with layer upon layer of urine-soaked straw beneath them. The younger children had been kept in cages, nearly starved and dangerously dehydrated. All were too traumatised to speak.

Hesh and Stacey walked in behind them with a child's hand in each of theirs. The children shielded their eyes from the harsh lights of the hospital and the shock of being free.

Chapter

44

The following morning, Rocco called for a debrief meeting to be held in the canteen. She wanted to check that everyone was okay. She needed to see if any of the team wanted someone professional to talk to. They had a critical incident and trauma team on standby. Fortunately, they had rarely been used so far but remained available with just a phone call.

It was just after 06:00 hrs. A letter had arrived for Rocco via a courier. It was from the Paediatric Specialist Nurse at the hospital where Holly Knowles had been taken by the police helicopter crew. Maggie read the letter out loud in the meeting.

"Dear Lady with the beautiful black hair,

You don't know me but I've seen you on the TV when I've managed to sneak a look when they were out of the house. I wish I looked like you but no one has ever cared enough to help or show me.

I didn't want to hurt anybody. I promise I didn't. But they are my parents and made me do these things to help them get all of the children ready. It broke my heart every time. They are very sick people and I cannot live knowing that I have somehow played a part. And I have found my place in the house to end it all. Please stop them. Please find the children and save as many as you can. They are all nice kids. I can't live now. I have to die. I have to be punished for my part. I'm so sorry. Please tell them all how deeply sorry I am.

Annie Mountford"

The team looked at each other as Rocco exclaimed 'Jeez, this is the kid that Albie and Holly have mentioned in their statements. This briefing is over for today. Come on, all of you. We have to get back to that house right now.'

Once back at the house they split up, searching every room for the little girl called Annie. Hearing what she thought was a noise, Rocco ventured down a set of steps on the other side of the cellar entrance.

She jumped, as an old man appeared, seemingly out of nowhere and attempted to grab her face with his big thick hand. She kicked him hard in his stomach and he stumbled backwards. He was the pensioner she recognised as the Mountford guy who they had lost yesterday during the arrest. She thought she had overpowered him, but she was wrong, very wrong. He might be old, but he was strong and fit. Years of being in prison had taught him to always be one step ahead of the enemy. He'd had to keep himself strong and fit.

A huge closed fist reigned punches on her head from above. He moved down her face, clutching at her throat, trying to squeeze the life out of her.

She started to feel dizzy. She heard herself scream. Knowing full well that, if he got the upper hand, he would get away and she would die here in this lonely, horrible, dead house where such unimaginable misery had taken place. Despite her best efforts, he was too strong. He landed a knock-out blow. Rocco slipped into unconsciousness.

Mark Walsh had been, as usual, keeping his sights on Rocco but he'd been unable to find her anywhere for the last twenty minutes. Since she'd gone inside the house. Hesh and Stacey said that she must have been called back to Headquarters. Mark told them to go on ahead, that he would check inside to make sure she had left the building.

The huge house was eerily quiet now that the scenes of crime team had left and all the children had been removed. He felt like he was being watched as he made his way through the dingy, dark, flocked wallpapered corridors.

His radio crackled and his bodycam light flashed intermittently as he searched out every nook and cranny with his torchlight.

A noise. He'd heard something. Yes. He could hear a groaning coming from further along. Calling for back-up, he tiptoed down the stairs to where the sound was coming from. She was laying on the ground. Mark rushed over to her. 'Ma'am. Ma'am, wake up.'

He found her pulse. It was strong. She was still alive. He radioed again for assistance. '387, I need back up NOW. Officer down, officer down. Ambulance required immediately.'

As Mark confirmed the coordinates, he heard footsteps running away just a few feet from him. Two of his long dreadlocks had become trapped underneath Rocco. He gently lifted her head to free himself. 'I'm sorry about this Ma'am, but I have to go after that bastard. Help is on the way.'

Leaving his chief, he continued radioing for assistance as he followed the sound of footsteps. There, just ahead of him, was Lance Mountford. He knew it was him from the photograph in the briefing room at the station. Lance was bent over. He appeared to be injured. But as Mark moved towards him, Mountford stood up straight and bellowed out like a sergeant major. 'Get the fuck away from me. You'll never send me down, never. You have no idea what or who you are dealing with, boy.'

With that, the big old man collapsed and thudded heavily to the ground. Mark moved closer to check his pulse. He could already see that the man wasn't breathing. His eyes and mouth were wide open and his trousers were soaking wet. Mountford had undoubtedly suffered a major heart attack.

From the end of that corridor, two paramedics appeared carrying a stretcher, quickly followed by several armed police and two detection spaniels.

'Don't worry about him. He's dead. Follow me, boys.' said Mark, as he led them to where he had found Rocco.

The first paramedic knelt beside her. He recognised her from the many incidents that they had jointly attended. Calling her name, checking her pulse and then her breathing, he soon secured her airway and quickly placed an oxygen mask over her face. They gently lifted her onto a board and carried her up the short stairway.

'What happened here, do you know?' asked the first paramedic.

'I think she was attacked by that dead bloke over there.' answered Mark.

Rocco tried to open her eyes. She pulled the oxygen mask from her face and tried to speak. The paramedic calmed her and told her to save her energy, but she was insistent.

'I think I've found the girl.' she whispered, her voice hoarse from Mountford's attempt to strangle her.

Mark was listening. He was leaning in and trying to catch her words. 'What are you saying, Ma'am?'

Knowing his chief, he put his hand up and told the paramedics to stop. 'Just a minute. This is important. We're in the middle of the biggest global missing children discovery ever. Now just wait and let her speak.'

Barely able to get her breath, Rocco tried again. 'I heard a sound before he attacked me. Maybe it's the girl. It was coming from behind the black metal door and through the cellar. The old man tried to strangle me. He thinks I'm dead.'

'Okay, take her away. I'll deal with this from now on. Come with me, guys. I think I know where she means, I saw that door when I first came down here.' said Mark as he nodded to the paramedics.

They took Rocco away and the rest of the armed officers followed Mark into the cellar. By this time, the other scenes of crime officers and search and rescue teams had returned for further forensic evidence.

The house was being boarded up. A police cordon had been placed all around the property, including the perimeter of the land.

In the cellar, the dogs were whining and scratching at the black metal door. Four of the biggest officers used crowbars to rip the door from its hinges. They discovered a small cubby hole.

There, on a concrete plinth lay the fragile body of a young girl. Her nightdress gave her a translucent appearance. The atmosphere was thick as officers rushed to the child's side. Please, please don't let her be dead, thought Mark as he was the first to reach her. There was a pulse. Yes, a pulse. Weak, very weak but it was there. 'Fucking hell, she's alive, guys! She's alive! We've got to get her out of here. Get out of my way.' he cried out.

He didn't wait for the paramedics this time. Mark picked little Annie up. She was as light as a feather. He cradled her to his body to keep her warm. The other officers formed a shield around him as he carried her out of the hell hole, up the stairs, through the house and outside to a waiting ambulance.

Maggie and the others were watching from three monitors back at the office. She hadn't been home very much in the last few days, only to feed her cats, change her clothing and to check her own house. She was unashamedly crying as she watched the professionalism and deep compassion of her work colleagues as they carried out their jobs so proficiently.

Trenchie had already got up and left when he'd seen Rocco had been injured. He was on his way to the hospital to find her.

Every single moment was being recorded and would all stand as evidence against, not only the Mountfords but against each of the other child abusers involved. No one was going to escape justice.

Rocco was taken straight into the hospital to be triaged. She was drifting in and out of consciousness. Trenchie was already waiting at reception, ready to be by her side once she had been assessed, treated and moved to recovery.

As she regained consciousness, she felt her hand in Trenchie's. She swiftly lifted both her hands to her head to try to soothe the pain.

The room she was in was very bright so Trenchie got up and turned the main light off. With just the natural light coming in through the window, she smiled at him.

'I thought I'd lost you'. said Trenchie.

'Thanks for coming, Trench.' she answered.

A doctor arrived to see her. Trenchie excused himself. 'Look I had better get back to the mayhem. You take good care okay and I'll see you later on.' said her boss.

As he was leaving, he nodded to Mark Walsh as they passed in the corridor.

Seeing a doctor with his Chief Inspector he waited until she was alone. Entering the room with his head around the door he said,

'Hey Ma'am. Are you doing alright?'

'Oh, hello Mark. What are you doing here? Is everything okay?'

'Well, it was me who found you after that old man attacked you. Do you remember what happened? I just wanted to make sure you were okay.'

'Well, I felt a bit woozy but the doctor has just said I can go home as long as I take a few days off from work.'

Mark raised his eyebrows knowing full well that that wasn't going to happen.

'I suppose I could work mostly from home, now we've got the children back.'

'Do you need a lift home? It's on my way.'

Chapter

45

The forensic archaeologists were working on several sets of human remains. Many more small skeletons were being found in the grounds of Magpie House. The last count stood at fourteen.

They had painstakingly recovered, collected and catalogued all the human remains, in preparation for them to be tested and identified and put into evidence. Each piece was proof that these young children had existed. The evidence recovered meant that they were able to piece together many other unsolved missing children cases, giving families some measure of closure. Some families had waited in agony for over eighteen years, never knowing the fate of their child.

A coroner had ordered the removal and storage of any skeletal remains. Every scrap of fabric, anything that might lead to the identity of the victim and how they died was to be recovered and documented. It was an all hands on deck operation. Each person was also required to wear a bodycam so that the minutest piece of material could be recorded and the chain of evidence secured. Everything was to be transported from where it was lying to a designated mortuary, pending further enquiries.

The officers and technicians working in the cellar of Magpie House were highly trained crime scene investigation specialists. They had continued to gather as much biological evidence as possible. They found blood, body fluids, hair and other tissue, crucial evidence in identifying the human remains. It was like being on the set of a horror movie.

Each team knew that they were working for the coroner, to obtain as much evidence as possible to enable him to determine the cause of death. The parents were foremost in their minds as they carefully and methodically collected every fragment of proof. This was physical and soul-destroying work. As a result, they were debriefed after each shift.

It was impossible to be hardened to what had happened in that house of horrors, especially for any team members who had children of their own. Many tears were shed, mercifully hidden by their protective face coverings.

Any clothing or footwear worn by the team also had to be bagged for identification and elimination. The police photographer also carefully documented any scenes before any work could take place.

DNA swabbing took place wherever possible, all of which had to be recorded onto a huge spreadsheet while still on scene. This case was unprecedented in its size and complexity. New ways of working were introduced to ensure the very best outcomes for building a case against the Mountfords and the other perpetrators, some known, others yet to be identified.

Officer Joel Davidson was the Senior Crime Scene Investigator and it was his job to establish the scene dimensions and to identify potential safety and health hazards. He was concerned that some of the early evidence may have already been compromised by the search and rescue team when they had first arrived on the scene. . Of course, he knew and understood that the preservation of life took priority. However, to avoid any further disturbance, he had secured the scene from the minute he arrived. Now, the whole area was cordoned off by yellow tape and markers had been placed at every possible contamination site.

He had initiated a focal contact, a point zero, from which to radiate outwards, but this wasn't like a general crime scene or a burglary or even a singular murder. It was a unique and complex crime scene in every way and he had to work inch by inch to make sure it was as controlled and protected as possible.

The site was now limited to a single entrance, guarded by a 'doorman' in situ, whose job it was to document all crime scene personnel and anyone else entering or leaving the scene. He was quick to thwart any attempts by unauthorised individuals to get on site. The media was kept well away. He took his role in establishing boundaries and maintaining crime scene integrity very seriously.

Working with his colleagues, Joel planned, communicated and coordinated the next steps. Firstly, they developed a theory about what may have occurred and relayed their theory through the cameras to the coroner's office administration team. Once they had a working theory about what might have happened, the investigators were able to anticipate other evidence that might be in existence. At this point, they had no idea just how many bodies were present.

Their enquiries extended to gathering information from witnesses and persons of interest. This intelligence allowed the CSI team to develop an evidence collection strategy, taking into consideration the weather conditions at the time of death, the season and time of day, as well as many other factors. Temperatures at the scene, odours, and positions of shade, length of darkness, doors, cages and purpose-built walls were included as evidence.

Joel was the best when it came to laser light technology which revealed fingerprints on the walls and other surfaces. Luminol, a substance that fluoresces on contact with blood was used to find as much DNA as possible. He had expertise in blood pattern staining and blood analysis, which could determine whether a victim was standing still, walking or running at the time of death. Sadly, he believed that most of these deaths were the result of sustained abuse and neglect rather than by a single episode of violence.

Moira, the photographer was old-school. She'd been doing her job for over thirty years. She liked Joel. He made sense to her, unlike several of the other jumped-up idiots she had to deal with. He was good at cutting through the red tape and endless protocol and politics. Like her, he believed in getting the job done as quickly and efficiently as possible.

Together they had worked out a scene plan. She had collected all the evidence required, which entailed detailed documentation with both her digital and video camera. The force had recently purchased a 3D scanner, which she'd put to good use. She had created sketches and diagrams that would be crucial for positioning and maintaining the best possible evidence for when it came time for court.

Moira knew she would be asked to attend the secondary review. She was looking forward to completing this job. It was hard on her and she could see her colleagues flailing with each new discovery.

Officer Davidson had also drafted in three of the best known forensic archaeologists to work on the numerous small human remains. This delicate and meticulous work would continue at the forensic laboratory.

Joel was on the telephone to his Head of Department, pleading with him to watch the camera footage. He was exasperated as he tried to convince the person on the other end of the phone that this was their best chance of obtaining the best evidence from this horror of a crime scene. They needed more resources if they were to work through the incredible volume of work. They needed the best and they needed them now. At last, Joel turned off his phone and threw it into his kit bag, with surprising accuracy.

The on-site search was finally over. It had taken ten days of around-the-clock work. The various teams left with a multitude of evidence bags which had to be carefully catalogued and cross-referenced. All of the evidence would now be used in the upcoming series of court cases. He was proud of his part in putting these vile excuses for human beings behind bars, hopefully for the rest of their miserable lives.

Chapter

46

It was known in the sexual deviant world as a child farm. It held regular auction days. The children would be auctioned off to the highest bidders and taken away, but the paedophiles were unable to keep them in one place for too long. The risk of exposure was too great. And so after a time, the children would be returned to the stinking prison until they were called for again. They would be abused again by the same perpetrator who would come to the farm, or resold to another bidder at a future auction.

It had been the biggest discovery of missing children and the largest child trafficking case ever to be uncovered and prosecuted in global history.

For several weeks after the huge discovery, every member of the Galaxy Unit, especially Maggie Seed, continued to visit the hospitalised children. They brought toys and gifts at every visit until the missing children were safely back home with their families.

Each of the surviving children had all been reunited with their families.

Holly Knowles was living with her mother. But now, they had a full-time live-in carer so that Holly could live her childhood and work on recovering from her horrific ordeal. She was receiving intense trauma therapy and it was helping her massively.

Leon Dalton was safely at home with his parents and wider family. He had initially found it difficult to leave his house for any reason. He too was receiving ongoing therapy. His mother had needed therapy and support for the guilt that she carried for leaving him alone for those few fateful minutes in the woods and then for trusting that awful man in the cottage. Her marriage to Leon's father failed, as was not uncommon in such cases. Now, her life revolved around keeping Leon safe and well. She bought him a puppy which he named Max. For now, he was content with that.

Harris Evans was returned to his family, who ensured he had a stable and consistent home life. He stayed friends with Leon and they kept in touch regularly. His parents kept up the friendship with Heather Knowles in and out of the group setting.

Clara Thompson was safe at home. She hadn't remembered much after taking the milkshake from Paul. After a long holiday with her father's family in Jamaica, Clara slowly started to rebuild her confidence, and eventually returned to her passion, ice skating. The following spring she won the Junior Skaters Gold Competition.

Patrick Ward was collected by his father Paddy who wrapped him in his arms as he lifted him into their transit van. The two Staffordshire bull terriers lathered him with slobbery kisses. They had missed their usual licking frenzy with Patrick. Gentle Herod muzzled his big soft nose into his neck when he got close enough. On the second night back, Patrick snuck out to the stable and nestled in to sleep with his equine friend.

Albie Raven's life quickly returned to normal and he continued with his well-loved sports. His father took him to their holiday home in Austria for a whole month so that he could concentrate on his skiing, see some of his friends and generally get back to being a young boy again. What happened never really left him though. He was fine in the daytime but at night he would often ask to sleep in the same room as his mum or dad. They could only hope that his fear of the night would resolve over time. He was fully engaged in long term trauma therapy. He had decided that he would like to become a therapist when he was older.

Annie Mountford could never quite believe that she had survived the life she'd had for so long. She had recovered from the drugs overdose. However, she often complained of a sore tummy. Cosmetic surgery to repair her cleft lip had been successful. Rocco had secretly paid for the private surgery. Annie was being fostered with a family in Loch

Lomond, Scotland, with the possibility of permanent adoption.

Her new home was a far cry from where she had been kept prisoner all of her life. It would take significant rehabilitation for her to even begin to live normally. But she was going to get all the help she needed. Rocco would make sure of that.

Annie's foster parents were Marie and Darren Channing. They had been visiting and keeping in touch since her discovery at Magpie House. She was going to be living with three other adopted children of a similar age and would go to school to work towards her chosen career. This would ensure that she would have the skills and confidence to forge her own way in life. Trauma counselling was expected to continue for several years. It would be a challenging time, but she was safe, at last.

Several of the parents had formed a 'post support group' for themselves and for their children to meet up and have picnics and days out together. It was the nearest they could get to normal. Any activities for the survivors of Operation Saturn were heavily supported by the government and local authority due to the number of perpetrators being social workers and other government employees.

Rocco had discussed being part of the group with Albie, but they both decided that they didn't want to get involved in the group work. She believed that it would cause further trauma if her son was constantly reliving what had happened. She and Mike paid for private post-trauma therapy for him and it seemed to be working. He was becoming his old confident self again, back to playing football and swimming. He pestered his father to go on skiing holidays, which his father always indulged during the school holidays. The family never let him out of their sight again.

Chapter

47

The case had finally been brought to court, Sixteen months later, and the judge made a statement: *Work is on-going to support the victims and make sure they have the best possible chance of a normal life ahead. I would like to pay tribute to their bravery throughout this process.*

He added*: I would also like to pay tribute to the professionalism and dedication of the police and emergency personnel who have worked tirelessly to bring this case to court. Not only was this a large and complex investigation but also one that involved working through a substantial amount of video evidence in which these perpetrators had recorded their horrific crimes. Our goal is to see these men and women behind bars today and for many years ahead.*

There was absolute silence in the Callachen Crown Court as the horrific details of the abduction, imprisonment and abuse that the paedophile ring had carried out on young children from the ages of four to ten years old had been read out in open court. The judge had continued his summing up.

"One of the most disturbing aspects of this case is that all of these children were simply taken from the streets, from their place of safety and from where they normally played, walked or carried out their everyday activities".

A report in the Callachen Times some eighteen months later described the sentencing and court duration.

"Twelve members of a paedophile ring who were caught in the act of an auction to sell children off to the highest bidder have been jailed collectively for ninety-six years. The trial that went on for three and a half weeks has finally ended.

The majority of the children who were discovered at Magpie House had been kept in a dark and dingy cellar. Countless historic remains of children who had not survived had also been found.

This nightmare had come to light after an intensive fourteen-month investigation. Eight men and four women from all over Europe were sentenced at Callachen Crown Court Monday, November 30th, having been convicted

on numerous counts of rape, abuse and torture of children aged under thirteen. They were also convicted on several counts of child trafficking, abduction and imprisonment.

At the centre of the Auction Network were Mr Lance and Mrs Gloria Mountford. He is now deceased. At the time of arrest, Mrs Mountford was the Chief Executive Officer of Social Services Safeguarding Children Department. She had been in that position for several years".

Mark Walsh's expert forensic examination of Gloria Mountford's computer and other devices, revealed that she had a secret file of the names and addresses of the recipients and buyers of the child auctions. He had found invoices for the storage and upkeep of the children imprisoned there while waiting to be auctioned or as storage for paedophiles without such facilities. Walsh found evidence of the couple's online marketing campaign for their Access Auctions, which were held several times a year. They were always held at Magpie House but were simultaneously streamed to a global audience of like-minded groups and individuals.

Telephone records from the Magpie House number showed the calls between the Mountfords and many of the abusers who were part of the

Access Auction. These were discovered during the police investigation known as Operation Saturn.

The defendants were convicted by a jury of eight men and three women.

Gloria Mountford: convicted of conspiracy to rape a child, conspiracy to commit sexual activity with a child, arranging and facilitating a child sex offence and possession of indecent images of children, as well as perjury, procurement, child trafficking and imprisonment. She was jailed for twenty-four years, with an extended licence for six years.

Lance Mountford: was convicted posthumously as it was evidenced not only by those who suffered at his hands but also by the signed confession of his wife. He was found guilty of eighty-six offences, including forty counts of rape of a child, sexual assault of a child under the age of thirteen and twenty-three counts of causing or inciting a child to engage in sexual activity. In addition to these offences, he was convicted of child trafficking and imprisonment.

Richard Murphy: convicted of conspiracy to rape a child under thirteen and conspiracy to commit sexual activity with a child under thirteen. Kidnap and imprisonment, of making indecent images of a child, and causing or inciting the child sexual exploitation of a fourteen-year-old. He was jailed for ten years, with a five year extended licence. Richard had signed a statement in the hope that the judge would be lenient if he gave the other parties names. He told how he had initially started to take children to abuse himself but then decided he would make money if he could procure them, to sell on to his former cellmate and his wife. He confessed to all of this and explained how the couple kept the children in their mansion called Magpie House. They collected them like jewels, like a magpie in its nest, shining brightly in the darkness below the house.

Paul Horton: convicted of procuring a child for sexual activity, abusing a position of trust, and conspiracy to engage in sexual activity in the presence of a child. He was sentenced to eighteen years and six months.

The other adults arrested at the scene were given similar convictions and prison terms. Further investigations are ongoing, against each of the defendants.

The investigation, has been the largest ever conducted by any team in the English police force. The Galaxy Unit was highly commended for their role in bringing these paedophiles to justice. There are more suspects yet to be investigated and work continues to bring them to court.

At a press conference, DCSI Edward Trenchard was the first to speak.

"This was an extensive inquiry which resulted in the sharing of intelligence with many other agencies and safeguarding leads. Not one stone has been left unturned by the scientific forensic archaeologists in the search to identify the remains of many other children who have tragically died at the hands of these people, whether by physical harm or severe neglect.

Further investigations are ongoing and my team will continue to seek out those who have been wholly responsible for these appalling crimes. Never before has such a large number of missing children and paedophile involvement been detected at such a rate. My team and I will continue to do what it takes to protect the living victims and to bring those responsible for these despicable acts to justice.'

The Mountfords, who are at the centre of this investigation, heartlessly exploited children for their own sexual gratification and for the many who attended the child auctions. The sentences they received reflect the disturbing nature of their actions. Given their collective ages, it is doubtful they and their co-abusers will ever be free".

Christina Morrison, long standing in her position as the Senior Crown Prosecutor for the Callachen and Drovedon Crown Prosecution Service (CPS) also gave a statement.

"This case involved the severe and unrelenting sexual abuse of vulnerable young children by a gang of active paedophiles. The young age of the victims greatly increases the seriousness of the offences.

As a result of the continued efforts and hard work and meticulous investigations of the Galaxy Unit and the strength of the evidence, four of the defendants pleaded guilty and fourteen more are yet to stand trial, once more evidence has been gathered to prosecute them.

The young victims have been both courageous and brave in their evidence disclosing the full extent of the depraved behaviours of those convicted and those yet to be.

We know that we cannot rewind the last two years for them and nothing can change what they have been through.

However, I hope that the convictions and sentences will give them, with the passage of time and appropriate support, at least a small sense that justice has been done. My thoughts are very much with them at this time."

Ongoing investigations into the small skeletons that were found in the grounds of Magpie House were still ongoing. The last body count stood at thirty-four.

These human remains and documentation on the computers found at the property had led to more than three hundred other potential offenders being identified as a result of Operation Saturn.

The Galaxy team and other detectives continue to work within a multi-agency system to hunt down and identify the individuals involved to protect any further children from such abuse.

Passing sentence, the Judge Mr Justice George Normanton said:

'This case, involving all of you and countless others, has caused extensive revulsion, disbelief and a longstanding aftershock. Your influence, Gloria Mountford, can only be described as callous and brutal in your depraved and relentless crusade to locate large numbers of vulnerable children to become engaged in sexualised behaviours.

You kept them in disgusting conditions and, in many cases, left them to rot and die. It is despicable. I am not sure that I have the powers to give you the morally correct sentence.

It is beyond the understanding of decent people how the minds of you and those who were involved have been capable of such heinous crimes and such depravity.

This is, in fact, the most frightening, sick and twisted case of child abuse I have ever had before me and I will seek to give you all the maximum possible sentences.'

Chapter

48

At just over eighteen months after the case had been completed. The courts were still sitting for others that were due to be held. DCI Rochelle Raven stood tall as she waited in line, prepared to receive the honour of the Queens Police Medal. It is awarded for gallantry or distinguished service and she would be entitled to use the post-nominal of MG after her name.

The work carried out in locating not only the recent missing cases of children but scores of cold cases was endless. Each one opened up a new one or led to the discovery of yet another paedophile ring and associated network. Although fourteen members of the paedophile gang, including Gloria Mountford, had already been convicted, the court cases and further convictions in the aftershock of this discovery would go on for years to come.

Hesh, Mark, Stacey and Nate were all in line for commendations for the extent of their investigative work and an additional honour was to be awarded to Maggie for her commitment, continuous efforts and involvement in the case.

Rocco's family stood side by side in the front line to witness the honours before them. Rocco's siblings stood with her ex-husband and Albie.

Mike was, as usual, impatient about her commitment to her job but still so very proud of her and her tenacity to stick with things until the very end.

Chapter

49

After the awards ceremony, the team and their families were due to attend the unveiling of the new Memorial that honoured the children who had died in the horrors of Magpie House.

On the way, Rocco and Albie needed to make a detour. Hospitals weren't her favourite place but as they walked into the children's unit at Harbury Queens Medical Centre for Excellence, Rocco couldn't hide her delight when Annie Mountford smiled at them as they walked into the ward.

'Hello, Annie. How are you doing?' asked Rocco reaching for the young girl's hand.

'I'm okay. Thank you, Mrs Raven. My mouth is a bit sore though but they say it will all heal beautifully. I can't believe that I can smile.'

'I'm so glad you made it, Annie. I was worried about all the children in that house, but especially you.' said Albie, holding her other hand.

'I'm so sorry, Albie. Sorry that you had to be a part of all that. I wish you didn't remember me only because of that place and how I was, how I treated you. It was because I was so afraid of them too. The only reason they didn't use me in those dreadful auction parties was because they said I was so ugly.' cried Annie.

'You are beautiful, Annie. And I know how kind you were to my son. If it wasn't for you, little Holly would never have escaped. We wouldn't have put all the pieces together and I would never have received your letter. Goodness knows what else would have happened if we hadn't found those children in time. And we would never have found you. Your bravery and courage go far beyond any award possible. I hope you will be happy in Scotland. You know, don't you, that if you ever need anything, anything at all, you can call me, okay.' said Rocco, handing her a card with hers and Albie's mobile number written on the back.

'Thank you, I will Mrs Raven. And you Albie, you take care, won't you?' replied Annie.

'There is one question I would like to ask you Annie.' said Albie. 'Why did they call the house Magpie House, do you know?'

'Yes. My father always used to say that magpies can and do take whatever they want. They can steal another's joy and get away with it. It's quite a sick comparison, really!' answered Annie.

They each hugged and said their goodbyes. Rocco and Albie left the hospital, happy to be leaving the nightmare behind them. Annie wasn't permitted to leave the hospital to go to the memorial opening because of the potential for infection in her wound. She wanted to go on her own, when her new foster parents collected her. She wanted to have that new memory in her mind forever. And she needed to be alone to do that.

Chapter

50

In April 2018 the Callachen Council, Police, Safeguarding units and thousands of people from the general public, funded a memorial to the children who had been held captive, as well as to those who had lost their lives in the horror that went on in Magpie House.

The property had been razed to the ground within six months of the forensic and coroners teams completing their investigations.

The new and very well thought out memorial had included designs from the children who were found alive, the parents' group, and also from the local schools and education services.

It was now a huge play area. One corner was set in trees to create a woodland theme. It was where the ashes of the eighteen deceased children were scattered. In between the trees, in random places, were bronze sculptures of children set deeply into the ground. They were happy figures, their faces laughing and looking up to the sky or kneeling as if to look at something interesting on the ground. It was truly beautiful.

In another corner of the ten-acre plot, a skate park had been built. The outside wall on the left contained the names of the lost children. Each name was inscribed onto a bronze and marble plaque. Each plaque was adorned with a small stainless steel butterfly.

A stunning lake had also been constructed in the centre of the site which had been filled with fish. New lily pads were already starting to grow which, in turn, attracted frogs and dragonflies, a myriad of colourful insects and butterflies, ducks and swans and so much more. One hundred trees had been planted around the perimeter.

A huge fountain had been placed in the centre of the lake, which lit up at night in a rainbow of colours. It wasn't only the children who visited to run and play, but dog walkers, joggers and cyclists.

Everyone in the vicinity and visitors to the area seemed to treasure the park. It was a respectful and solemn place. One which honoured the children who had lost their lives and offered a place for peace and reflection for the families involved.

It was also a joyous environment. An acknowledgement to those children who had survived and a place where future generations of children could play with each other and their families for many years to come. It was a memorial to the children but also a testament of triumph over evil. A place of comfort and hope.

Glynis Solomon came from a long line of angry, broken females. She had fought every day of her young life, to survive the regular outbursts of her violent, whiskey-drinking, alcoholic mother. Barely coping psychologically, she was dragged through the social care system, confused and afraid as her silent rage simmered.

Available from Amazon Online and all

Major High Street Book stores

suejdaniels.com
stonefacepublishingltd.co

Book 1

The Salvaging of Sonny Chapman is the first of three novellas telling the story of a young mother from Derbyshire, England. Sonny works as a portrait artist, commissioned by the bereaved relatives of those whose loved ones have died. As Sonny sketches the eyes of the portraits she works on, she starts to hear their voices, just as if she is having a conversation with them.

Available from Amazon Online and all

Major High Street Book stores

suejdaniels.com
stonefacepublishingltd.com

Book 2

The Restoration of Sonny Chapman is the second book in the trilogy. Sonny's life has changed from violent chaos and her very near death to a more peaceful and safe place. In the stunning setting of her new husband's birthplace, the beautiful ancient backdrop of Tuscany, Italy, where his world and family have entwined with hers.

Available from Amazon Online and all

Major High Street Book stores

suejdaniels.com
stonefacepublishingltd.com

Book 3

The Journals of Sonny Chapman is the third, and final, book in the trilogy. Now, with three full journals in the family, Mirabella, wise beyond her years, sets up her room in the Cat's Eye Clinic. She starts to feel danger and senses the energy of a mysterious presence.

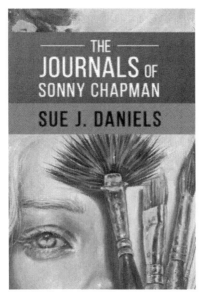

Available from Amazon Online and all

Major High Street Book stores

suejdaniels.com
stonefacepublishingltd.com

Short Story Book

Courting with Strangers

Courting with Strangers is a series of six short fictional stories that are all associated with court cases in the UK and Europe. They each beautifully showcase the background experience behind each conviction and subsequent sentencing outcomes – Some of which, could happen to any one of us.

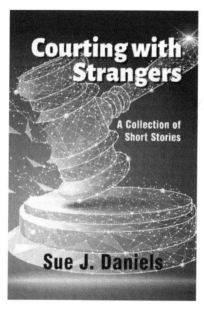

Available from Amazon Online and all

Major High Street Book stores

suejdaniels.com
stonefacepublishingltd.com

Short Story Book

The Energy of Love this series brings together flash fiction of audio short stories, centred on lost loved ones and how an energy connection between them and those left behind, can often alleviate and comfort in grief and loss. Mist in the Morning - A beautiful story of profound energy showcasing how love can continue, even between two worlds, just separated by an invisible veil.

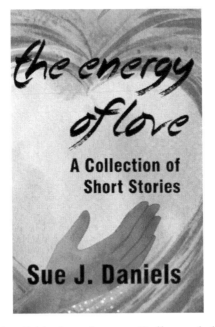

Available from Amazon Online and all

Major High Street Book stores

suejdaniels.com
stonefacepublishingltd.com